Mandie Mysteries

Mandie's Cookbook

MANDIE
AND THE
MYSTERIOUS FISHERMAN

Lois Gladys Leppard

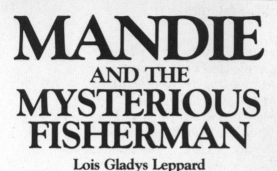

BETHANY HOUSE PUBLISHERS

MINNEAPOLIS, MINNESOTA 55438
A Ministry of Bethany Fellowship, Inc.

Mandie and the Mysterious Fisherman
Lois Gladys Leppard

All scripture quotations are taken from the
King James Version of the Bible.

Library of Congress Catalog Card Number 91–77739

ISBN 1–55661–235–4

Published by Bethany House Publishers
A Ministry of Bethany Fellowship, Inc.
6820 Auto Club Road, Minneapolis, Minnesota 55438

Printed in the United States of America

This book is especially for all those many, many
readers who have expressed a desire to join a
fan club. For information write to:

Mandie's Fan Club
Post Office Box 5945
Greenville, South Carolina 29606

About the Author

LOIS GLADYS LEPPARD has been a Federal Civil Service employee in various countries around the world. She makes her home in Greenville, South Carolina.

The stories of her own mother's childhood are the basis for many of the incidents incorporated in this series.

Contents

"Judge not, and ye shall not be judged; condemn not, and ye shall not be condemned; forgive, and ye shall be forgiven."

Luke 6:37

Chapter 1 / The Mystery in Antwerp

"You know, it was worth almost drowning in Germany to get Rupert to reform," Mandie said to Celia and Jonathan as they strolled along the wharf in Antwerp, Belgium. Snowball, her white kitten, walked at the end of the red leash Mandie held.

Her two friends quickly stopped to stare at Mandie.

"You don't really mean that!" Celia Hamilton exclaimed.

"Rupert was not worth it. You could have drowned," Jonathan said.

"But I didn't fall into the lake on purpose, remember?" Mandie said. She glanced back up the walkway to be sure they were staying within sight of her grandmother, Mrs. Taft, and her friend, Senator Morton. The adults were too far away to overhear the young people's conversation.

"I know. It was an accident," Celia said as the three walked on.

"Right," Mandie said. "It was an accident, but it was

also the cause of Rupert finally coming to his senses and straightening up and—"

"Yes," Jonathan broke in, "just long enough to fish you out of the lake. He's probably back to his old sneaky tricks by now."

"But he apologized to us for all the mean things he had been doing," Mandie protested. "And I know he talked to his grandmother about everything, because I happened to pass the library and heard them discussing it."

"He knew he'd better mend his ways enough to save you or he might've been blamed if you'd drowned. He was the only one anywhere near the lake when you fell in," Jonathan reminded her.

Celia asked, "Do y'all think his grandmother will allow him to marry Lady Catherine even though she has no money, which they need so badly to renovate the castle?"

Mandie's blue eyes sparkled as she said, "I believe the baroness will agree to their marriage because, first of all, they are definitely in love, and because Lady Catherine does have a title, and those things seem to be so important to these Europeans."

"I myself see no use for such things, but over here they're important," Jonathan agreed. "I'm glad the United States is not that way."

"Oh, but some families in the United States do try to pick out their sons' and daughters' marriage partners," Celia said.

"Well, no one is going to pick out my husband for me if I ever decide to get one," Mandie said, quickly tightening her hold on Snowball's leash as he tried to jump ahead.

"Since that is usually done for money in the United States, you won't have to worry about it," Jonathan teased. "Think of all the wealth you'll inherit someday."

"Jonathan Guyer!" Mandie exclaimed, stopping to give him a sharp look. "Money doesn't mean a thing to me as long as I have something to eat and wear and a place to live. Money can't make a person happy and you should know that."

Jonathan immediately became serious as he said, "You're right. I have firsthand knowledge of that. Maybe if my father didn't have so much money, things would be better between us."

"He'd certainly have more time to spend with you," Mandie agreed. "Maybe he realizes that now since he thought you had been kidnapped when we found you." The three walked on.

"Senator Morton promised to discuss things with him," Celia added.

"Just consider yourself lucky to have a father, Jonathan. Remember Celia and I have both lost our fathers," Mandie reminded the dark-haired boy.

"Yes, I know," Jonathan said, walking faster. Snowball tried to pull loose from Mandie's grasp on his leash. "Watch that cat. We don't want to have to chase him all over Belgium. After all, we're only going to be here a few days." He grinned his mischievous grin.

"Mandie, I am so grateful to your grandmother for allowing me to come along on this trip to Europe with y'all," Celia said. "I've really enjoyed all the countries we've been in."

It was the summer of 1901 and the girls had come to Europe with Mrs. Taft during their vacation. Senator Morton, a family friend, had escorted them.

"I have, too," Mandie said. "But it will soon end, and we'll have to return home and go back to school." She sighed.

"We have had some interesting adventures," Jonathan said. "So far, we've been able to solve all the mysteries we've become involved in."

"And we still have Holland, Ireland, and what other countries Grandmother decides to visit, and then back to England," Mandie said.

"And onto that huge ship again to go home," Celia added. Turning to Mandie, she said, "I think we're pretty well traveled for thirteen-year-olds."

"I think so, too, until I remember all those private schools in all the different countries that Jonathan has been attending all his life," Mandie said, smiling at Jonathan.

"But I'm also a year and five months, lacking four days, older than you are," Jonathan teased.

Celia smiled and said, "And I'm three months and five days older than Mandie."

"Oh, for goodness' sakes, y'all try to act so old—sometimes," Mandie said, putting on a serious air. She glanced back to see where her grandmother and Senator Morton were. They weren't on the walkway behind them. "Where did Grandmother and Senator Morton go?" She stopped to gaze around.

Celia and Jonathan immediately looked for them.

"And we promised we'd stay within their sight," Celia said.

Jonathan suddenly pointed across the roadway. "There they are, over there looking at the merchandise in that vending cart."

The girls then saw the adults.

Mandie breathed a sigh of relief as she pushed a wisp of blond hair under her bonnet with one hand and held tightly to Snowball's leash with the other. "I sure am glad we didn't lose them. We might get lost."

"Yes, since we only got here this morning," Celia added.

"But I've been here before. I won't let us get lost," Jonathan promised.

"Grandmother made it clear that we weren't to get out of her sight," Mandie reminded him. Then smiling she added, "She wants to be sure we don't get involved in another adventure."

"So if we happen to run into another mystery, we can't pursue it," Jonathan said, grinning mischievously.

"Well, things will probably be better when Uncle Ned gets here," Mandie said. "She trusts him to watch over me because he promised my father he would when my father died."

"But he wasn't sure about when he would catch up with us after we left him in Germany," Celia said.

Uncle Ned, the old Cherokee Indian, had been Mandie's father's friend. And he had always turned up when Mandie needed him. He was not really Mandie Shaw's uncle and was not really related to her, but Jim Shaw had been one-half Cherokee. Mandie was proud of her Indian heritage and often visited her Cherokee relatives in North Carolina. Uncle Ned managed to follow Mandie on this journey to Europe, and he kept in touch with her through the different countries she visited with her grandmother and her friends.

"He knows how long we'll be staying here, so he'll be sure to arrive sometime soon," Mandie said.

Suddenly Snowball jerked the leash out of her hand and raced toward the water where several boats were docked. The three young people raced after him.

"Snowball! Come back here!" Mandie called to him, holding up her long skirts as she ran.

Celia and Jonathan were right behind her. The kitten slid to a stop as he pressed his front claws into the floor of the old wooden pier. Then leaping into the air, he landed in one of the small boats. The men working around the boats yelled at him in a foreign language that Mandie couldn't identify, and she realized Snowball wouldn't understand what they were saying either.

"He's American," she called to the man. "He can't understand you." She reached the edge of the pier and stooped to see how she could rescue the cat from the boat.

"Look at what he's doing!" Jonathan exclaimed. "That's a fishing boat and he is trying to get to the fish."

Mandie couldn't suppress a smile as she watched Snowball trying to push up the lid of a huge basket on the boat. Then she frowned and yelled at him, "Snowball, come here! Right this minute!"

The workmen had stopped work to stare at the young people. Then one of the men stepped over into the fishing boat and looked down at the cat.

He called to them in French and Jonathan understood and replied. The man carefully scooped up Snowball and stepped out to hand him to Mandie.

"What did the man say, Jonathan?" Mandie asked. She grabbed her white kitten and held him up to look into his blue eyes. "You naughty kitten!"

"He just said for us to be still and he'd catch the cat, and I thanked him," Jonathan explained.

"Oh yes, thank you!" Mandie called to the man who took off his hat and waved it at them.

"Snowball, I'm not going to carry you everywhere we go. You are going to behave and walk on the leash like you're supposed to do," Mandie told him. "Do you understand?"

Snowball meowed sadly and pushed his head against Mandie's chin, purring loudly. Mandie set him down and wrapped the end of the leash around her wrist.

"He thought he was going to get a free fish dinner," Celia laughed.

"And those men would have put a stop to that," Jonathan said.

Mandie looked around the pier. "Jonathan, are these all fishing boats docked here?"

"I believe so," Jonathan said. "Let's walk along the water and look at them." He led the way and the girls followed. They stopped to look at each boat.

When they came to a curve in the shoreline, they found no more fishing boats. But Mandie looked ahead and spotted another boat in the distance.

"There's one more," she said. "Let's go that far and then come back."

"That may not be a fishing boat, Mandie, because it's isolated from the others here," Jonathan said as the three walked toward the distant vessel.

As they came nearer, Mandie looked at the peeling paint on the small boat and the dirty windows in the tiny cabin.

"It looks like it's deserted," she told her friends. "I don't believe it's being used for anything."

"It sure looks dilapidated," Jonathan commented as they crowded close to the edge trying to see inside.

"It seems to be just flopping around in the water and not properly tied up," Celia said.

Mandie looked around for some way to get onto the boat. Its side rose high enough that they couldn't just step over into it. And there didn't seem to be any steps or ladder to board it.

"How can we get into it?" she asked her friends.

"Mandie, we might fall into the water," Celia cautioned her.

"Look at the deck," Jonathan said. "Some of the

boards are hanging loose. I'd say from the condition of that boat, it has been abandoned a long time."

The girls looked where he pointed. The wood seemed to be old and rotten.

"Well, I'd still like to look inside," Mandie insisted as she picked up Snowball and walked around. Turning to Celia she held out Snowball and said, "Would you hold him for me? I'm going to see how close I can get."

"Mandie, please be careful," Celia warned as she took the kitten.

Mandie moved cautiously to the edge of the pier. There was no railing to hold on to, only the old wooden planks of the floor to keep her from falling in. Jonathan followed closely behind her. Celia stood grasping Snowball and holding her breath as she watched at a safe distance from the edge.

Suddenly there was a loud moaning sound that seemed to be coming from inside the boat. Mandie and Jonathan stopped in surprise.

"What was that?" Mandie whispered to the boy.

"Whatever it was, I'm sure it must have come from the boat," Jonathan replied.

The two stood there for a moment waiting and listening. The sound didn't occur again. They edged their way forward. Mandie could feel the old planks shake and move beneath their feet. She reached for Jonathan's hand to steady her.

"I don't think it will fall in," Jonathan said, looking down at the floor. "It's just old and wobbly."

At that moment the moaning sound came again— then silence.

"Do you think someone is inside the boat and is hurt or something?" Mandie said softly.

"It could be some kind of animal if the boat has been

deserted," Jonathan replied. "Let's see if we can get nearer."

The two slowly moved toward the last plank of the pier. As Mandie watched the boat bob slightly up and down in the water, she became dizzy-headed and tightly squeezed Jonathan's hand and closed her eyes.

"I think I'd better go back," she admitted as she turned around.

"We'll have to figure out some other way to get near the boat," Jonathan decided as he held her hand and they slowly made their way back to where Celia waited.

"I'm glad to see y'all made it back," Celia remarked.

Suddenly a loud moan filled the air and then ceased. The young people looked at one another.

Mandie turned back toward the boat. "Jonathan, there is someone on that boat and they sound like they're dying or something. We need to find out what's wrong," she said, starting to walk back out on the pier.

"Wait!" Jonathan said, quickly grasping her hand. "We have completely forgotten something—your grand-mother and Senator Morton."

"Oh goodness, you're right!" Mandie exclaimed as she looked around. The area they were in seemed to be deserted. "We'd better find them at once!"

She took Snowball in her arms and led the way back in the direction they had come. Her friends quickly fol-lowed. Finally they reached the street where the vendor's cart was and where they had seen the adults. There was no one there except the vendor now.

"Oh, Jonathan, can you ask that man if he knows which way my grandmother went?" Mandie said.

"If he speaks French I can," Jonathan replied, hur-rying toward the man who was sitting on a small stool behind his cart.

The girls waited and watched. Mandie knew the man evidently understood Jonathan's French, as he stood up and waved to his left up the street. Jonathan hurried back.

"He said they walked that way," Jonathan said, pointing the same direction the man had.

"Oh, I hope we can find them. My grandmother will be furious with us," Mandie said as they hurried up the street.

They walked so fast they went right past Mrs. Taft and Senator Morton, who were at a shopwindow, without even seeing them.

"Amanda!" Mrs. Taft called.

Mandie turned quickly back and saw her grandmother and rushed over to her.

"It's time to get back to the hotel," Mrs. Taft said.

"Yes, Grandmother," Mandie said breathlessly as she looked at her friends. Evidently they had not even been missed.

"This way," Senator Morton said, motioning to the cross street.

The adults walked ahead and the young people followed at a distance where they could talk. They huddled close together as they went.

"Whew! That was pure luck!" Mandie murmured with a shake of her head. "How are we going to get into that boat? We've just got to find out who or what is inside it making that terrible noise."

"Here we go again, Mandie," Celia warned her. "Your grandmother said no more adventures, remember?"

"Well, this is not exactly an adventure," Mandie protested as she held Snowball tightly in her arms. "There may be someone on that boat who needs our help."

"We don't even know what plans your grandmother has, so we can't decide on when or how we're going to return to that boat," Jonathan reminded her.

"The only thing I know for sure that Grandmother is going to do is visit an art museum somewhere in Antwerp. I don't believe she has any friends living here to visit," Mandie told them.

"Then if she doesn't have any friends to visit, that means she will want us with her everywhere she goes," Jonathan said.

"Maybe she and Senator Morton will want to go somewhere without us," Mandie said hopefully.

"Mandie, couldn't we just tell your grandmother we think someone is in that boat and needs help?" Celia asked.

"No, no, no!" Mandie quickly replied. "She would just say she'll get the police to investigate and then forbid us to go there."

"If you think she would forbid it, then we shouldn't go," Celia said.

"Well, I'm not sure she would," Mandie replied. "But I don't think she'd mind if we helped someone in distress."

"Mandie, it would depend on who it is and what is wrong," Jonathan told her.

"But we won't know that until we find out what's going on in that boat," Mandie insisted.

Celia sighed and looked at her friend. "I think we're going to get into trouble again."

The three had walked so slowly that the adults had stopped for them to catch up.

"Amanda, let's move a little faster. I don't know about y'all, but I feel like having some food," Mrs. Taft said as they came up to her and Senator Morton.

"Food! That's for me," Jonathan agreed with his mischievous grin.

"Yes, ma'am," Mandie replied. "I just realized I'm hungry, too. Where are we going to eat?"

"In the hotel, dear," Mrs. Taft said. "Tomorrow we'll rent a carriage and go sightseeing. We'll find some interesting place to eat then."

The three young people exchanged glances.

"Will this sightseeing take all day, Grandmother?" Mandie asked as they walked on.

"Why yes, dear. That's what we came for, so y'all could see the town," Mrs. Taft said, stepping forward beside Senator Morton.

Jonathan made a silent groan upon hearing that. Celia smiled. But Mandie said softly, "Don't worry. We'll figure out a way to get back to that boat."

"If you say so," Jonathan replied.

Chapter 2 / Robbery

The next morning after a hearty breakfast, Mandie and her friends and her grandmother waited in the reception room of the hotel where they were staying while Senator Morton went out to engage a carriage for a day of sightseeing.

"Grandmother, could we just walk around in the lobby till Senator Morton gets back?" Mandie asked as she stood up from the settee where she and Celia and Jonathan had been sitting opposite Mrs. Taft. She held Snowball by his leash.

Celia and Jonathan quickly looked at Mandie and then at her grandmother.

"No, dear, you will all stay right here and stay seated until the senator gets a carriage for us," Mrs. Taft replied emphatically, pointing to the settee.

Mandie quickly sat back down by her friends. "I just figured we'd be sitting most of the time in the carriage and my legs feel like they need some exercise," she said.

"We'll get plenty of exercise getting in and out of the carriage and walking around the places we plan to visit," Mrs. Taft replied. She kept watching the doorway for the senator to return.

Mandie sighed softly and glanced at her friends. Celia smiled and Jonathan made a face and shrugged his shoulders.

"What are we going to see, Mrs. Taft?" Jonathan asked.

Mrs. Taft turned to look at him. She smiled and said, "I'm not very well acquainted with Antwerp, but Senator Morton is and he knows where to go and what to see. We will visit one art museum."

Mandie sighed to herself and grimaced. She knew absolutely nothing about art and was not really anxious to learn. To her a picture was a picture. Some she liked and some she didn't. This place called Antwerp didn't seem to be very interesting. Except for the abandoned fishing boat down by the pier and its moaning and groaning sound, she thought the city was boring.

"Daydreaming?" Celia whispered.

Mandie took a deep breath and smiled. Her blue eyes twinkled. "I suppose I'm just getting tired of this European trip. When we run out of mysteries to solve it gets boring."

"I agree," Celia said softly.

"Don't give up," Jonathan muttered under his breath. "We'll get back to that old boat somehow."

Mandie had watched her grandmother during their whisperings. Mrs. Taft had not seemed to hear or notice. But she knew her grandmother well enough to know that the lady would drag them to every nook and cranny in the city before they journeyed on to the next country. The tour of Europe was considered part of their education, Mrs. Taft had informed them, and she didn't intend letting them miss a single important place.

"Watch out!" Jonathan suddenly called to her.

Mandie's hold on Snowball's leash was lax, and the kitten chose that moment to dart away from her grasp. He quickly disappeared into the adjoining lobby. The three young people ran after him.

"Amanda! Don't let that cat get away!" Mrs. Taft called after them as they went through the doorway.

"Snowball, you come back here, do you hear?" Mandie yelled at the fleeing white cat.

Snowball glanced back at his mistress and quickly ran through the open door of the elevator nearby. The only person Mandie could see inside it was a short dark man who was carrying what looked like a large piece of cardboard. The man evidently didn't even see the cat or the young people as the door closed and the elevator began its journey upward.

"Oh, just wait till I get my hands on you, Snowball!" Mandie exclaimed as she watched the elevator leave.

"Half a second earlier and I could have held the door of the elevator," Jonathan groaned.

"I don't know why that man inside didn't see Snowball," Celia said.

"Celia, would you please go tell my grandmother what has happened, and I'll run up the steps to try to catch him when the elevator opens," Mandie said.

"Sure, Mandie," Celia said and hurried back toward the reception room.

"Come on," Jonathan said, quickly rushing up the nearby staircase.

Mandie raised her long heavy skirts and ran after him. The two were out of breath as they looked at the indicator for the elevator on that floor.

"It didn't stop here. Come on. Next floor," Jonathan said, racing up more steps.

Mandie caught up with him, and they were both annoyed to see by the indicator that the elevator was still traveling upward.

"How many floors does this hotel have?" Mandie asked, trying to catch her breath as she turned to follow Jonathan up another flight of stairs.

"Four. This is the top floor," Jonathan gasped as they arrived at the elevator.

The elevator was just stopping as they rushed up. Mandie could see through the glass door that the man was still on it. As it opened the man cautiously stepped out, looking first to the left and then to the right. As he saw the two young people standing there, he quickly looked down the long corridor. At that moment Snowball raced out behind him and got in his pathway. The man raised his foot to kick at the cat.

Mandie and Jonathan immediately realized what the man was planning to do and they rushed forward and knocked the man down. The large cardboard he was carrying slid across the hallway. Mandie snatched up Snowball.

"Don't you dare kick my kitten!" Mandie yelled at the man as he got up from the floor and hurried to pick up the cardboard.

"I did not kick that cat," the man said in British English as he straightened up with the cardboard in his hands. He was quickly examining it.

Mandie watched. It wasn't a piece of cardboard, after all. It was some kind of painting. She could see one corner of the picture where the cloth covering had slipped off. It was a green color.

"You planned to kick that cat. We saw you," Jonathan told him.

"It's good you didn't because you would have gotten a lot worse from us," Mandie added.

"And I tell you that you are lucky you didn't damage this," the man said haughtily, tucking the painting under his arm and hurrying down the corridor.

"I'd sure like to know who that man was," Mandie commented as they watched the man walk away. Then she noticed he was not going to a room on that floor but had run down the staircase instead. "Now isn't that stupid? Why did he come all the way up here on the elevator and then go back down the steps?"

"Come on, Mandie," Jonathan urged her. "Maybe he pushed the wrong button or something. Anyway, we'd better get back downstairs to your grandmother."

"I hope she's not too upset with Snowball," Mandie remarked as they went down the stairs.

The two reached the ground floor in time to glimpse the man going out the front door of the hotel. He was still carrying the painting.

"That man certainly acts strange," Mandie commented as they watched him leave.

"Mandie, Jonathan, the senator is back and we're ready to leave," Celia called to them from the doorway of the reception room.

Mrs. Taft and Senator Morton appeared behind Celia.

"Amanda, please, please hold on to that cat or you will have to leave him in your room when we go out," Mrs. Taft told her.

"But, Grandmother, the maid or someone might let him out if I leave him in my room," Mandie protested as they all walked toward the front door. "I'm sorry. I'll be more careful with him." She had carried the kitten down the stairs and continued to hold him in her arms as they went outside and entered a carriage waiting for them.

Once inside the vehicle the two adults began their own conversation. So the young people discussed the man with the painting. Celia had seen him leave the hotel.

"Maybe he was a stranger in town and got in the wrong hotel," Celia suggested.

Mandie thought for a moment and then agreed. "That could have been the reason he left. And he did speak English with a British accent."

"He had a British accent, but I don't think he was British," Jonathan disagreed. "There was a slight twang to his speech, as though he had learned the English in England but was really some other nationality."

Mandie's blue eyes opened wide. "Well, aren't you smart, Jonathan Guyer? I never would have caught that twang, as you call it. But then I'm not familiar with other languages like you are."

Mrs. Taft spoke to them. "Are y'all watching the scenery as we travel along? Look at all the beautiful trees and flowers. There's an interesting building." She pointed to a huge structure with ornate carvings. "Senator Morton, would you please tell us what you know about the city?"

"I'd be glad to," Senator Morton said, smiling at the three young people. "That particular building is one of the government offices. We are on our way to the square in the main part of the city. There you'll see some really old and beautiful architecture."

Senator Morton continued on and on. As Mandie gazed out the window, her mind traveled back home. She wondered how her mother was, and her little baby brother, and her Uncle John who had married her mother when her father died. And, oh, how she'd like to see Aunt Lou and Liza and Jenny and Abraham—all who worked for her Uncle John and all her very dear friends. She wondered when Uncle Ned would arrive in Antwerp.

"Grandmother, do you have any idea as to when Uncle Ned will get into town?" Mandie asked as soon as Senator Morton took a moment to catch his breath.

"No, dear," Mrs. Taft said as she turned to the senator. "Have you received any message from him?"

"No word at all, but then I don't expect to because he said he would catch up with us as soon as he could," Senator Morton said.

"I know he had to stop to see some friends after we left the castle in Germany, but we aren't going to be here very long, and I was hoping he'd hurry up and come," Mandie complained as she held tightly to Snowball in her lap.

"I'm sure he will, dear," Mrs. Taft replied as their carriage came to a halt.

Mandie looked out to see the square that the senator had told them about. It was old and beautiful in its own way, but she had seen so many squares in Europe that they were all beginning to blend in together in her mind.

They alighted from the carriage and the adults led the way around the square. Mrs. Taft cautioned the young people not to get out of her sight.

"We've been through so many difficult situations since we came to Europe that I insist for the rest of your visit all of you are to stay within my sight," Mrs. Taft told them as they walked past shops of various kinds.

"Yes, Grandmother," Mandie replied.

"Yes, ma'am," Celia and Jonathan added.

The three drifted along behind the adults, and finally at noontime Senator Morton found a pleasant little sidewalk cafe where they could rest and eat. Mandie tied Snowball's leash securely to the table leg.

After having Senator Morton translate the menu for them, all the young people decided on "just some scrambled eggs and rolls," as Mandie said.

Mrs. Taft immediately looked anxiously at the three young faces. "Y'all are not sick, are you?"

The three smiled and Mandie said, "I'm just tired of food that I'm not used to. I'd really love to have some grits, with the eggs, and some of Aunt Lou's hot biscuits."

"Me, too," Celia agreed.

"And I'd like to have some of that good old New York food, just anything so long as it's cooked back home," Jonathan remarked.

"Maybe you three can eat more tonight then," Mrs. Taft suggested, turning to Senator Morton with her order.

"I've never had New York food, Jonathan," Mandie told him. "But I don't imagine it could be as good as our food back home in North Carolina."

"It's every bit as good and probably better, but I haven't had any of your southern food, so I don't know for sure," Jonathan replied, a mischievous grin lighting his face.

"So you've traveled all over the world practically, but you've never been in the southern part of our own country. Shame on you," Mandie teased. "You're going to have to come and visit. And we'll take you to see my Cherokee kinspeople."

"I plan to one day, but you know how it is with my father so tied up in business deals all over the world. I have to go to school wherever he sends me," Jonathan said.

"Jonathan, I do hope your aunt and uncle in Paris come back home soon so you can go stay with them awhile after we all go home," Celia told him.

"I do, too," Jonathan said, and turning to the senator he asked, "You haven't heard anything from my father, have you?"

"No, I'm sorry to say, I haven't," Senator Morton replied. "We'll probably hear from him before we leave Belgium."

Mandie and Celia had met Jonathan on their way to England when they came to Europe. His father was always too busy to allow the boy to stay home in New York and go to school there, so he was sent from one private school to another in various countries. Senator Morton had contacted Mr. Guyer and asked permission for Jonathan to visit awhile with his relatives who were working for a newspaper in Paris. So far no decision had been made.

After everyone had finished the noon meal, Mrs. Taft decided it was time to visit the art museum.

"Now that we've eaten and rested awhile, shall we go on to the art museum?" she asked Senator Morton.

"I was going to suggest the same thing," he said, smiling as he assisted her to rise from the table.

Their carriage had waited at a nearby corner, and as they walked toward it the young people drifted behind to talk.

"Maybe this art museum is the last place for today and we can go back to the hotel to rest," Mandie whispered to the others.

"I think I know what kind of resting you'll be doing," Jonathan teased.

Mandie smiled at him as she held Snowball in her arms and said, "I'll rest for a while and then I'd like to go for a walk down on the wharf."

"And back to that old dilapidated boat," Celia added.

Mandie nodded. "I'd just like to see it again and figure out a way to get on it."

"I think I know how," Jonathan said softly.

"Amanda, Celia, Jonathan, get a move on now," Mrs.

Taft called to them as she waited by the carriage ahead.

The three hurried forward.

"Tell me how," Mandie said under her breath.

"Soon as I get a chance," Jonathan promised.

Once they were all inside the carriage, Senator Morton gave the driver instructions to go to the art museum. It took only a few minutes to get there. The vehicle came to a stop in front of a small plain-looking building.

"This is the museum?" Mandie questioned as the three young people left the carriage behind the adults and looked around.

"Yes, dear, this is a private museum that has some priceless treasures," Mrs. Taft told her.

As they neared the front entrance, Mandie noticed a large group of people evidently waiting to go inside.

"Is it open, Grandmother?" she asked.

"Oh, goodness!" Mrs. Taft said as she looked about and turned to the senator. "Is it open? Why are all these people here?"

"I'll check," Senator Morton said, quickly leaving them to go ahead and speak to the guard at the entrance. He returned to inform Mrs. Taft that the museum was open now, but it had been closed all day because of a robbery early that morning.

"A robbery!" Mrs. Taft exclaimed. "What was stolen?"

"It seems one of Peter Paul Rubens' oldest paintings was missing when they opened this morning. But they've finally decided to let people in, so it shouldn't take us long to get inside."

"A Rubens!" Mrs. Taft exclaimed. "It must be priceless!"

The three young people had listened with interest upon hearing a mystery surrounded this museum. They quickly discussed it in whispers among themselves as they waited in line.

"A painting!" Mandie said. "That man in the elevator had a painting with him and it was all wrapped up."

"Oh, Mandie, that doesn't mean he stole it," Celia said.

"But he acted strange, Celia," Jonathan told her.

"Yes, like he was afraid someone was following him or something," Mandie whispered. "And he was a mean person, too, because he intended to kick Snowball." She held her kitten close to her.

"Too bad we didn't follow him to see where he went," Jonathan said.

"No way we could've done that with Grandmother waiting for us," Mandie said softly as they moved forward in line.

Mrs. Taft looked back.

"We're right behind you, Grandmother," Mandie assured her with a smile.

"Be sure you stay there when we get caught in the squeeze at the doorway," Mrs. Taft told her and then turned back to converse with Senator Morton as the line moved forward.

Once they got inside the museum, it was hard to see anything because there seemed to be so many people and all of them taller than Mandie and her friends.

"Let's find the place where the Rubens should be," Mrs. Taft told Senator Morton, and then she turned to look back at the young people. "Don't lose us now."

Mandie and her friends followed, and when Mrs. Taft and Senator Morton finally stopped, Mandie tried to see what they were looking at. Evidently a large piece of muslin had been draped over the spot where the Rubens had hung. There were other pictures surrounding it. Mandie edged closer, and when she managed to get in front of everyone else, she reached over the rail and flipped the muslin out from the wall. The bottom of it was loose.

"Look!" she whispered to her friends. "You can see the outline of where it was hung, and it wasn't a very big painting at all."

Jonathan and Celia silently agreed.

"Amanda! What are you doing?" Mrs. Taft quickly asked as she saw Mandie flipping the muslin. "Don't touch that!"

A strong male voice from behind her added, "Do not touch!" Mandie glanced back to see a guard watching. She smiled at him and said, "Sorry, I just wanted to see how big it was."

The guard did not smile as he repeated, "Do not touch!"

"We apologize," Mrs. Taft said to the man and then urged the senator on down the line, adding to the young people, "Come along now."

"You're going to catch it when we get out of here," Jonathan whispered to Mandie.

Mandie didn't answer but walked along behind her grandmother. Celia followed.

When Mrs. Taft finally decided it was time to go, the three young people followed her and the senator back to the carriage. On the way Mandie and her friends discussed the missing painting.

"I believe the painting the man had in the hotel was the same size as the one that's missing," Mandie declared in a whisper.

"I agree," Jonathan said.

"Well, I didn't exactly notice what the man had so I don't know," Celia added.

"I think we have another mystery we may be able to

solve," Mandie said, smiling at her friends. "All we need to do is find out who that man was that we saw and where he went."

"That's impossible, Mandie," Jonathan said under his breath. "But knowing you, you don't believe in the word 'impossible,' do you?"

"That's right," Mandie said, her blue eyes twinkling. "We can always find a way."

Chapter 3 / An Argument

Mandie was hoping to get a chance to ask Jonathan how he thought they could get on the abandoned boat, but when they arrived at their hotel, Mrs. Taft immediately spoke to Mandie.

"Amanda, please come to my suite. We have something to discuss," Mrs. Taft told her as they walked along the corridor.

Mandie silently groaned. She knew what the discussion was to be about.

"Yes, Grandmother," she said, and turning to Celia she told her, "I'll be there in a few minutes." She smiled at Jonathan, who was following Senator Morton on down the hallway to their suite.

"Let me take Snowball," Celia offered and reached to get the kitten from Mandie. She went on into the rooms she shared with Mandie.

Once inside Mrs. Taft's suite, Mandie took off her bonnet and ran her fingers through her blond hair. She knew her grandmother could be stern sometimes.

"Sit down, Amanda," Mrs. Taft told her as the lady also removed her bonnet and sat on the settee beside Mandie.

"I'm sorry, Grandmother. I know what we are going to talk about. I shouldn't have fiddled with that piece of muslin in the museum," Mandie quickly said, watching her grandmother's face.

"You are exactly right," Mrs. Taft said, frowning. "You must learn to grow up and act like a young lady. You are entirely too impulsive, Amanda. That was embarrassing for the guard to speak to you like that."

"Please forgive me, Grandmother," Mandie said with a hint of tears in her blue eyes. "I am really and truly sorry. I guess I haven't been around people like you long enough to know what to do and not to do. My first eleven years with my father were in the mountains where everyone acted natural and didn't have to worry about what other people thought." She said all this in one breath.

Mrs. Taft looked at her and reached to hold her hand. "I keep forgetting you were denied the better things in life because your father took you and went to live with that woman in the hills," she said.

Mandie immediately jerked her hand from Mrs. Taft's and stood up, her blue eyes full of anger.

"My father married 'that woman,' as you call her, because you separated my mother and father because he was part Cherokee, and you didn't want your daughter married to a 'half-breed,' and you told lies to my mother and—" Mandie was almost screaming at her grandmother.

Mrs. Taft quickly stood up and tried to put an arm around Mandie, but Mandie moved away from her.

"I know, I know, dear," Mrs. Taft interrupted her. "I am

to blame, and I will regret my actions the rest of my life, but you can't undo deeds you've done. I can only hope you have forgiven me. And I do try to be a real grandmother to you because you are my real granddaughter, no matter what your heritage is—"

"My heritage is part Cherokee and you try to ignore it but it's the truth," Mandie said with a tremor in her angry voice. "I want to go home to my mother!" She broke into loud sobs and ran for the door.

Mrs. Taft tried to stop her. "Amanda, we must forgive each other. We can't hold grudges. Amanda!"

Mandie was fumbling with the door handle and finally got it open. She raced outside and down the hallway to her room. Mrs. Taft stood in her doorway watching.

Mandie almost knocked Celia down as she pushed open the heavy door to their rooms.

"Mandie! What's wrong?" Celia asked in alarm.

Mandie ran into her bedroom and sat in a big upholstered chair by the window. She hugged her knees and bent her head as she shook with sobs. Snowball tried to get on her lap as he loudly meowed.

"Mandie!" Celia said, following her into the room. "Can I do anything? Tell me, Mandie. What happened?" She stooped in front of her friend.

Mandie ignored her and sobbed on.

"Look, there's something wrong, I can tell, Mandie," Celia insisted as she tried to reach for her friend's hand, but Mandie swiftly curled up away from Celia. "Mandie, I'm your friend, you know that. We've always shared all our secrets and sorrows. Please tell me what's the matter with you. I want to help. You are my dearest friend, Mandie." Celia watched closely.

Mandie took a deep breath, trying to control the sobs, then hiccupped loudly. She wiped her tears with the hem of her long skirt as she raised her head to look at Celia through tear-filled eyes. Celia was her dearest friend, and she had nothing to do with the distress Mandie felt now. It was unfair of her not to confide in Celia.

"I . . . I . . . my . . . my grandmother . . ." Mandie tried to speak as her voice quivered. And then quickly she said, "Celia, I want to go home to my mother."

Celia looked at her in surprise. "Why, Mandie? I thought we were having a good time over here in Europe. Tell me, why do you want to go home?"

"Because my grandmother said—" Mandie stopped as she found she just couldn't put the scene with her grandmother into words. She drew a deep breath and went on. "My grandmother and I had an argument."

"About the muslin in the museum that you lifted?" Celia asked, continuing to stoop in front of her friend.

Mandie nodded. "And other things. I want to go home to my mother." She straightened up in the chair.

Celia sat on the floor. "Mandie, I don't think you really want to go home to your mother right now. I think you're just mad at your grandmother about something. Remember what Uncle Ned always says. Think. Think things through. Think about every little detail. And when you do this, things won't seem as bad as you thought they were."

Mandie slid from the chair onto the floor and embraced her friend.

"Celia, you are so dear to me," Mandie told her. "I wish you were my sister."

"You are like a sister to me, too, Mandie, because I've never had a sister or a brother. You at least have a little brother back home," Celia said as the girls straightened up to look at each other.

"I know. I also remember being jealous of him. Oh, Celia, I think I'm really a bad person. I seem to do so many things wrong," Mandie said, leaning back against the chair as she sat on the floor.

"I do bad things too, Mandie," Celia said. "Even though I've always had my mother to teach and guide me through terrible situations, I don't seem to learn very well."

Mandie smiled at her friend. "Oh, Celia, you are an angel compared with me. I try real hard but I don't always behave as I should. Celia, do you think it's because I'm part Cherokee?"

Celia looked shocked at the idea. She laughed. "Mandie, where did you get such a crazy idea? Look at how good Uncle Ned is, and he's full-blooded Cherokee."

Mandie hung her head and said softly, "My grandmother hates the Cherokee part of me."

"That's why you were crying," Celia said.

"She made some remarks that I thought weren't fair," Mandie said, standing up and straightening her crumpled skirt. She decided she had said enough about the scene with her grandmother. "Let's see if we can talk to Jonathan. He was going to tell us how we could get on that old boat down at the wharf."

Celia also stood and said, "Mandie, there you go. We are expected to rest until it's time to go out for supper tonight."

"I can't rest. Besides, my grandmother didn't exactly say we had to rest. She said *she* was going to rest and that we would meet later for supper," Mandie told her. She tied on her bonnet and walked over to open the door. Snowball followed.

"Well, I suppose I'll go with you," Celia said, reaching for her bonnet and putting it on. "Are we taking Snowball?"

"Absolutely no," Mandie said, bending to pick him up

and going toward the bathroom. "I'll put him in here and shut the door. And hope no one comes in our rooms and lets him out."

The girls quietly walked down the corridor to the door of Jonathan's room. As Mandie lifted her fist to knock, the girls were surprised by Jonathan opening the door. Mandie felt him looking at her eyes, which she realized must be red from all that crying. She dropped her head.

"I knew you two would be along soon," Jonathan told them in a whisper. "Come on." He started quietly down the corridor.

"Where are you going?" Mandie hurried to catch up.

"Down to the wharf, of course," the boy said, with his mischievous grin. "Isn't that where you wanted to go?"

Mandie was surprised at his taking the lead. She was usually the one who decided matters of what, where and when, and how and why sometimes.

"Yes, but . . ." Mandie replied hesitantly. She had not really planned on leaving the hotel without her grand-mother's permission.

"Mandie, we shouldn't," Celia warned her.

"Well, I'm going with or without you two. I would have already gone down there but I was waiting for you," Jonathan said and began briskly walking on down the hall-way.

"Wait," Mandie called softly. She quickly followed him. Glancing backward she asked, "Celia, are you coming?"

"I suppose so if you are," Celia said, trailing behind her friend.

Mandie felt her heart fill with guilt at what she was doing. Her grandmother would be furious if she found the girls missing. But then maybe they could solve the mystery of the sounds coming from the old boat, and someone might be helped in the process. Besides, her grandmother was already angry with her. And though she tried to ignore it, she knew she was still angry with her grandmother.

"Come on," Jonathan called to the girls. He waited at the top of the steps going down into the lobby.

Mandie and Celia caught up with Jonathan, and the three hurried down the stairs and out the huge front door of the hotel. Once outside Mandie breathed a sigh of relief. No one had seemed to notice them.

"Jonathan, we'd better make hay while we can," Mandie urged. "I have a feeling we're going to be missed."

Jonathan grinned mischievously at Mandie and asked, "Make hay? What does that mean? We're in a city, not in a hayfield somewhere." He stopped in front of the girls.

"Oh, Jonathan, come on, let's get going. You know what I mean," Mandie replied with a sigh as she rushed on down the sidewalk.

"No, I really don't," the boy insisted as he followed.

Mandie gave him a suspicious look and walked on.

Celia explained. "What she means is, we'd better hurry while we can."

"That's right, Jonathan Guyer. We'd better get a move on," Mandie told him as she started toward the wharf.

"Talking about foreign languages, I do believe you have your own foreign language," Jonathan teased.

Mandie stopped to look at him. "Are we going to the wharf or not?" she asked.

"Of course we are," Jonathan said. "Come on."

As the three walked on, Mandie said, "I'll remember to pick at what you say, too."

Celia slowed her steps to ask, "Are we going in the right direction? I thought that boat was down another street. I don't remember being on this one."

Mandie and Jonathan also stopped and looked around.

"You're right, Celia," Mandie agreed. "I think we came one street too far."

"Then all we have to do is go back one block and go down the next street," Jonathan said as he turned back the way they had come.

The three walked several blocks, trying different streets, before Mandie finally spotted the vendor with the cart where they had stopped the day before.

"Now I know where we are," Mandie said with a sigh of relief.

"Yes," Celia agreed.

"And we should go that way," Jonathan said, pointing.

By the time they finally came within sight of the boat, Mandie realized they had wasted a lot of time trying to find it. She was worried that her grandmother would come to their rooms and find them gone. And she would not only be upset with Mandie but would be worried since she wouldn't know where they were in this strange city.

"We've got to hurry," Mandie urged her friends as she lifted her long skirts and ran the rest of the way to the pier. Celia and Jonathan followed.

They stopped near the end of the pier and looked at the old boat rocking in the shallow water.

"All right, Jonathan, how did you figure to get on the boat?" Mandie asked.

Jonathan picked up some pieces of old timber lying at the edge of the pier and carried them to the end of the boardwalk.

"Like this," he said, stacking up the wood. "Then we get some more and keep adding to it until we've made an extension that will reach to the edge of the boat."

"I'm not sure that would be safe," Mandie said, surveying what he was doing. "Won't the wood all tumble off the end of the pier and into the water when we step on it?"

"I don't think so," Jonathan said, straightening up to look at the wood.

"I think it will," Celia said.

"Let's heap it all up and then try it," Jonathan said, quickly gathering up more scattered timber and placing it with the first pile.

"You know I can't swim, Jonathan," Mandie said, backing off. "I'm not about to try it. You go ahead if you want to, not me."

"All right then, I will," Jonathan said. He finally had a network of boards that formed an extension to the pier by jutting out over the water.

"Get back, Celia," Mandie warned. "Jonathan is going to fall in, and when he does he's going to make a big splash." She moved farther back and Celia followed.

"If the thing caves in, the boards are near enough to the boat that I can grab the edge of it to keep from falling into the water," Jonathan said, looking at what he had made.

"Well, hurry up, Jonathan. We've got to get back to the hotel," Mandie told him.

"Hold your breath, girls," Jonathan said as he slowly stepped on the pile of boards.

Mandie and Celia silently watched as he slowly put one foot in front of the other. He didn't seem to be scared, but the boards wobbled now and then. Finally he got near the outer end of the pile of old lumber.

"Ha, ha! It worked!" Jonathan called to them as he laughed and looked back. The loose boards suddenly flew out from under his feet, and he went flying in the air beyond the end of the pier. He grabbed for the side of the boat but couldn't quite reach it.

Mandie and Celia watched as he made a big splash in the water, just as Mandie had predicted.

Mandie laughed and called to him, "I told you so!" She knew Jonathan was considered an excellent swimmer, but she ran forward to be sure he got out of the water all right. He was clinging to the post under where she stood, and as she watched he began climbing upward, with water pouring from his wet clothes.

Celia moved closer and when Jonathan finally grasped the boards beneath their feet, the girls bent to give him a hand as he tumbled upon the pier. He sat there looking up at them as water continued to flow from his clothes.

Grinning he said, "Guess it didn't work."

"It certainly didn't," Celia said, shaking drops of water from her long skirt.

"I'll say it didn't," Mandie agreed. "Jonathan, can't you squeeze out some of the water so you can walk? We've got to get back to the hotel."

Jonathan struggled to his feet, his wet clothing clinging to him. He took off his jacket and tried wringing it out.

"I'll help," Mandie offered as she caught one end of the garment and helped him twist it.

"Y'all are going to ruin his jacket for good," Celia told them as she watched.

"Here, I'll just roll it up and carry it," Jonathan said, bundling up the jacket. He stomped his feet, then sat down and took his shoes off and poured the water out. "All right," he said, standing up, "I'm ready. Let's go."

They couldn't walk very fast because Jonathan was weighted down with the wet clothes and soggy shoes. The girls kept away from him because he continued to splatter water.

"Why don't you girls go ahead? I'll be along shortly," Jonathan suggested. "My feet just won't go any faster."

"I think we'd better all stay together," Mandie said. "You know, I was just thinking. We didn't hear any noise from that old boat a while ago, did we?"

Jonathan looked at her. "You're right. I don't remember hearing a thing."

"Neither did I," Celia added as the three continued up the street.

"Maybe whoever it was, or whatever it was, is not in the boat anymore," Mandie suggested.

"Or they heard us outside and were quiet," Jonathan said.

Mandie just happened to glance back as they went along. She stopped abruptly and said, "Look! Isn't that the man we saw in the hotel with the painting?" She pointed to a man in dark clothes who was going in the direction from which they had come.

"Where did he come from? He didn't pass us, I'm sure," Jonathan said as he watched the man.

"Maybe he came out of one of the shops along this street after we passed it," Celia suggested as she, too, stared at the man.

"Come on. Let's see where he is going," Mandie said, excitedly rushing off back down the street they had come up.

"Wait for me!" Jonathan called to her as he bent and removed his soggy shoes, then picked them up and ran after Mandie.

Celia hesitated between Mandie and Jonathan and finally hurried with Jonathan to catch up with Mandie.

"I hope he doesn't see us," Mandie said as she and her friends slowed down a short distance behind the man. "Isn't he the same one we saw in the hotel?"

"He looks like the same man," Jonathan said.

"I wonder what he did with the painting," Mandie said as they continued following.

At that moment the man hurried down an alleyway between two shops. The young people followed and then paused at the entrance to watch him. There seemed to be shops down the way, and the man looked as though he was searching for one in particular. He stopped to look at the front of each one.

Several people strolling along the sidewalk of the street stared at Jonathan's appearance. He stared back at them. His clothes were still sopping wet and he was carrying his shoes and jacket.

"Jonathan, you are attracting attention," Mandie said, smiling at the boy as she looked him over.

Jonathan glanced down at himself. "Didn't anybody ever see someone wet before?"

Mandie and Celia laughed. And at that moment when they weren't watching, the man disappeared.

"Where did he go?" Mandie asked as she gazed down the alleyway. "He's gone!"

"Well!" Jonathan exclaimed.

"He must have gone into one of those shops down that way," Celia said.

"Let's go see," Mandie said, hurrying down the alleyway and stopping to look in the shop near where the man was the last time she saw him. Jonathan and Celia followed.

None of the shops were enclosed in the front. Therefore it was possible to see right inside. The three quickly made their way to the end of the alley, but the man was nowhere to be seen.

"Oh, shucks!" Mandie exclaimed, stomping her foot. "We *would* lose him!"

"We don't know for sure whether he was the man from the hotel. We never did get close enough to see him straight in the face," Jonathan reminded her.

"But he looked like the same one," Mandie insisted. "He had on dark clothes like that man and he seemed to walk the same way."

"Whether he was or not we've lost him, Mandie, and your grandmother will be turning the hotel upside down looking for us," Celia reminded her.

"Oh, yes, we'd better hurry," Mandie agreed. The three rushed back toward the hotel. "We'll catch up with him sooner or later."

Chapter 4 / The Man in the Park

When the young people arrived at the hotel, they found the lobby full of guests wandering around. Mandie stopped just inside the door and whispered to Jonathan, "It must be time for supper."

"Yes," he agreed as he tried to slip through the crowd without attracting attention. But the manager saw him as he walked by the desk, and the man wanted to know what had happened.

"Oh, I just got a little wet, nothing serious," Jonathan told him, weakly smiling as he tried to go on.

"If you will give those wet clothes to the maid, we can clean and dry them for you," the manager told him.

"Yes, sir, I will," Jonathan said as he finally got past the desk.

The three hurried for the steps and went up them two at a time. By the time they arrived at their floor they were all panting for breath.

"See you later," Mandie called to him as she and Celia

went toward their rooms and Jonathan continued down the corridor to his.

Mandie rushed up to the door and then paused. "I'm afraid to open the door. Grandmother may be just waiting for me inside," she whispered to Celia.

"Then I will," Celia said, stepping forward to push open the door.

As the two looked inside they both sighed with relief when they found the rooms empty.

Mandie heard Snowball howling in the bathroom and rushed to let him out. She removed her bonnet and plopped down on her bed. They had two beds in the huge bedroom in this hotel.

"I think I'm worn out," Mandie said, lying back on a pillow. "Do you think we have time to take a nap?" She looked at the clock nearby on the table. "It's twenty minutes after five and Grandmother said to be dressed by seven. I think I'll take about thirty minutes of winks." She straightened out to get comfortable.

"I'm afraid I'd oversleep so I'll just write in my diary while you sleep," Celia told her as she went to her trunk in the corner and got out her journal. She propped up with the pillows on her bed.

"Ummm," Mandie replied as she dozed off. Snowball curled up at her feet.

Mandie dreamed of her father. She was living in the log cabin at Charley Gap. Her father, Jim Shaw, was putting up a rail fence around their property. Mandie was following him around and helping with whatever she could. She had been crying.

Jim Shaw took off the big-brimmed hat he was wearing, ran his hand through his curly red hair, and reached to put an arm around Mandie. His blue eyes looked down into hers.

"We must all love one another, my baby," Jim Shaw said as he squeezed her tight. "And we must forgive. I know it's hard to live right, but we have to try with all our might."

"Daddy! Daddy!" Mandie exclaimed as her eyes filled with tears. "I love you, Daddy!"

Suddenly Mandie woke to find Celia shaking her. Mandie rubbed her eyes and sat up. The dream of her father had been so real and now here she was in the hotel in Belgium.

"Mandie, you must have been dreaming," Celia told her as she sat down on the side of Mandie's bed.

"Oh, Celia, I was dreaming of my father. I wish I could go back to sleep and see him again," Mandie cried, her blue eyes brimming with tears.

Celia reached for her hand. "I know," she said. "You were talking to him in your sleep. I dream of my father, too, sometimes. It's a jolt to wake up and find that it was all a dream."

"He was telling me to forgive. It was just like he knew I had an argument with my grandmother," Mandie said, sitting up on the bed. "And, Celia, I've thought a lot about what happened to my mother and father because of my grandmother when she separated them. I suppose my father forgave Grandmother but, you know, he never even told me a thing about all that."

"I know. Uncle Ned told you about your Uncle John when your father died and then your Uncle John told you about your mother," Celia replied.

"I know I have to forgive Grandmother for what she said to me today, but it's awfully hard to figure out how to forgive," Mandie said, drying her eyes with the hem of her long skirt.

"The way I do it, Mandie, I make the decision to forgive

whoever it is and then I ask their forgiveness. But you really have to mean it when you do this. You have to feel in your heart that you can forget and that you won't let whatever it was come up in your feelings toward that person again," Celia said.

"That's hard for me to do," Mandie said. "I have to keep telling myself that I must forgive because I have done things, too, to other people. And I sure wouldn't want them to hold things against me for the rest of my life."

Celia stood up. "It's time we got dressed, Mandie." She looked at the clock. "We only have three quarters of an hour to be ready."

Mandie jumped off the bed and said, "I have to hurry because I want to talk to my grandmother before we go out to eat."

The girls chose clean dresses from the wardrobe and took turns in the bathroom. Celia allowed Mandie to go first so she could have time to see her grandmother.

Mandie quickly buttoned up her pale blue silk dress and tied the cream-colored lace Bertha collar at the front. She brushed out her long blond hair and tied it back with a blue ribbon, leaving the ends swinging free. Looking through her hat box, she selected a cream-colored lacy bonnet and laid it on a nearby table.

Then turning to Celia who was putting on a pea green silk dress, she said, "I'll be back in a few minutes. I'm going to see Grandmother."

"I'll wait here until you get back," Celia replied as she shook out her long skirt.

As Mandie opened the door to the hallway, she came face-to-face with a maid who was about to knock.

"Food for the kitty," the young girl said as she stood there with a bowl in her hand.

"Oh, thank you. Please put it in the bathroom for him," Mandie told her and hurried down the hallway to her grandmother's suite.

Mrs. Taft was so slow in answering her knock that Mandie was beginning to think her grandmother might have gone out. Finally she opened the door enough to see who it was. She just stood there looking at Mandie.

"May I come in, Grandmother?" Mandie asked. She noticed her grandmother was fully dressed and ready to leave.

Mrs. Taft didn't answer but opened the door wide. Mandie stepped inside. She thought her grandmother was acting awfully strange. The woman had not said a word but was evidently waiting for Mandie to explain why she had come to her grandmother's rooms.

"Grandmother," Mandie began hesitantly as she stood before her.

"Yes," Mrs. Taft said, waiting for Mandie to go on.

Mandie tried hard to ask her grandmother's forgiveness, but the words choked in her throat. Even though she knew she should put past acts of her grandmother out of her mind, she was numb and speechless. Mrs. Taft looked as though she was still angry with Mandie.

"Well?" Mrs. Taft said.

Mandie quickly swallowed and turned to leave the room. "Celia and I are ready to go," she said as she stepped into the hallway.

"All right, Amanda," Mrs. Taft replied. "As soon as Senator Morton lets me know we'll be by your rooms."

"Yes, ma'am," Mandie quickly said and hurried back down the hallway.

Mandie was angry with herself. Why couldn't she bring herself to ask for her grandmother's forgiveness? Her heart fluttered as she thought, *Am I becoming so hardhearted I can't forgive anymore? Oh, I need Uncle Ned to talk to! I wish he'd hurry up and get here.* And most of all she wished she could talk to her father again, even though in a dream. But then she remembered her reaction to her father's advice while she was dreaming. She had not answered him at all that she could remember.

Celia was waiting. Snowball was licking his paws after gobbling down the food the maid had brought. Mandie walked into the room and sat on a nearby chair. She didn't know what to say to Celia because she had not accomplished a thing by going to her grandmother's room.

"Grandmother will be by after us as soon as Senator Morton lets her know he is ready," Mandie remarked as she jumped up and walked around the room.

Celia looked at her friend and said, "I hope we go somewhere nice to eat, but I also hope they have food that I know what I'm eating." She laughed.

Mandie smiled at her, plopped down on the settee by her, and replied, "That will be one wonderful thing about getting back home, won't it? No one cooks like Aunt Lou and Jenny, and they have promised to teach me as soon as I have time."

"I know," Celia said, pushing back her long auburn curls. "My mother wants me to learn, too, someday."

"If we didn't have to go to school in Asheville and live there all the school year, we'd have a whole lot more time to do other things, wouldn't we?" Mandie said.

"Yes, but my mother says school is more important than anything else, especially Misses Heathwood's School that we board in," Celia replied.

There was a knock at their door and Celia ran to open it. Jonathan stood there, in fresh clothes, with his dark hair washed and dried, grinning mischievously.

"Oh, hello, I thought you would be Mandie's grand-mother," Celia told him as she pushed the door wide open.

"She and Senator Morton are on the way. I am to give you girls instructions to get your bonnets on. We're off to a restaurant somewhere," Jonathan said teasingly.

Mandie and Celia quickly put on their bonnets, straightened their long skirts, and joined Jonathan in the hallway after Mandie shut Snowball in the bathroom. They caught up with Mrs. Taft and Senator Morton down the corridor as they headed for the elevator. Although Mandie really preferred the steps since the elevator always made her stomach turn over, she didn't say a word as they all stepped inside. She looked at her grandmother, who seemed to have ears only for the senator as he discussed some sightseeing suggestions. Mandie held her stomach and closed her eyes as the elevator descended with a jerky motion.

The young people were silent until they went through the huge front door of the hotel. Then the senator told them, "The restaurant where we plan to dine is within walking distance so I didn't engage a carriage. We'll walk in this direction." He turned left up the avenue.

Mrs. Taft, alongside the senator, cautioned the young people, "Please be sure you stay right behind us now."

"Yes, ma'am," the three chorused.

"When do you girls want to go back to that old boat?" Jonathan asked under his breath.

"As soon as we get a chance," Mandie replied. "I have been thinking about how we can get on that boat and you know, I believe I remember seeing a rope hanging over the edge of it, do y'all?"

Celia shook her head. "No, I don't."

Jonathan thought for a moment and said, "You may

be right. With all that tumble I took I don't know for sure. What good would a rope on the boat do?"

Mandie said softly as she noted the adults were conversing between themselves, "If we could reach it we could swing on it over to the boat."

"If there is a rope it may not be secured at the other end, Mandie. Besides, I don't know how we would reach it," Jonathan said.

"If we could find something long enough to reach over and poke it, we might be able to pull it to us," Mandie said. "After all, the boat isn't that far away from the pier."

"I'm not sure it's possible but we can always try," Jonathan said softly. "But when?"

"If it isn't too late when we return to the hotel and if it isn't too dark, we could run down there and see what we could do," Mandie whispered.

"Mandie!" Celia said. "This is a strange town to us and we shouldn't go wandering around at night."

"You don't have to go, Celia," Mandie said, smiling at her friend. "I won't get mad."

"You know if you insist on solving things, I always have to go with you, just to be sure that you don't get in trouble for one thing," Celia said, laughing softly as she looked at Mandie.

The adults suddenly slowed down in front of them and Mrs. Taft turned back to say, "This is the restaurant. It's a well-known exclusive place so please be on your best behavior, all three of you."

The young people all chorused, "Yes, ma'am," and followed the adults through a fancy arched doorway into a huge dining room. Crystal chandeliers hung from the ceiling over white linen-covered tables. Massive green draperies covered the floor-length windows surrounding the room. At the far end three musicians were playing classical music.

The host showed them to a table near a window. Potted plants hovered around the room and created a little privacy for tables here and there. But when Mandie sat down she discovered she had a clear view of the other diners. Jonathan and Celia were seated on either side of her, with the adults across the table.

When Senator Morton translated the menu for them, Mandie was delighted to find the restaurant had listed fried chicken with hot rolls.

"Fried chicken!" she exclaimed. "I'll have that."

"Me, too," Celia quickly added.

"And I suppose me, too," Jonathan said. "It sounds like the best thing on the menu."

Senator Morton told them, "I'd better explain something to y'all. You know people in different countries don't cook like everyone else so you may not get what we called fried chicken back home."

"That's all right as long as it's chicken," Mandie said. "At least I'll know what I'm eating."

Her friends agreed. The senator and Mrs. Taft decided to try it, too. When the waiter had left with their order, Mrs. Taft looked at the young people and asked, "Did y'all get some rest this afternoon?"

"Yes, ma'am," the three chorused. Mandie dropped her gaze. Jonathan grinned mischievously and Celia smiled.

"Do y'all feel up to walking a mile or two after we eat?" Mrs. Taft asked. "Senator Morton says there's a beautiful park about that far up the avenue and I thought some exercise after eating would be good for us."

"A park?" Jonathan questioned.

Senator Morton explained, "Oh, it's full of things to do, swings, carousels, and trails through flower beds and that sort of thing. I think y'all would enjoy it." He smiled at them.

"Oh yes," Mandie agreed.

"That would be fun," Celia added.

"That's better than sightseeing," Jonathan said.

"Since you young people don't seem interested in exploring the city, I thought the park might get your attention," Mrs. Taft said, smiling at Jonathan. Then she glanced at Mandie. Mandie tried a feeble smile and then dropped her gaze.

When the waiter returned with the food, the young people were delighted to find the fried chicken was really fried chicken even though it did have a faintly different taste from what they got back home. And the rolls were delicious. The three ate as though they hadn't been fed in a week.

The host came by their table to check on their food, and Mandie told him, "This fried chicken is the best food I've had since I left home."

The tall dark-haired man smiled and said, "It is practically from your back home. Our cook is American. She married one of our men and came here to live."

"That's wonderful!" Mrs. Taft spoke up. "We'll have to come back again while we're in Antwerp."

"Yes, she does a lot of American cooking for us," the man said. "I appreciate that you enjoy it. I will tell her."

No time was wasted dawdling over food. The young people cleaned their plates and were ready to go. As soon as Mrs. Taft and Senator Morton were finished they left for the park.

There wasn't a chance to talk among themselves as they walked up the avenue because Senator Morton kept acting like a tour guide and pointing out famous landmarks along the way. With other plans on their minds the young people didn't absorb much of the information. But when they saw the park with its many attractions and beautiful flowers and shrubs, the three immediately became interested.

"We'll just walk around a little while, and then the senator and I will sit somewhere while you three enjoy the attractions," Mrs. Taft told them as she and Senator Morton led the group down a winding pathway.

Mandie and her friends were enchanted with the beautiful flowers, the fish ponds, the arched bridges over flowing streams, and the alcoves for sitting and resting.

"Oh, this is like a fairy tale!" Mandie exclaimed, following the adults.

"Yes, it is," Celia agreed.

"Since I don't read fairy tales, I wouldn't know, but I can see some swings and a carousel through the bushes over there," Jonathan said, pointing to their left.

Mrs. Taft turned back to say, "We're going in that direction but the pathway is winding. The senator and I will rest on some seats over there and you three may swing or ride the carousel. But please remember, you are not to get out of our sight, is that understood?"

"Yes, ma'am," the three agreed.

As they came into the opening Mandie and her friends hurried ahead to the swings. Mrs. Taft and Senator Morton sat down nearby within view.

"Let's ride the carousel first!" Mandie said excitedly, hurrying toward the man who was assisting riders.

Jonathan and Celia agreed. They all got on and then scrambled onto the wooden horses as the machine started turning and the music began playing.

Mandie felt light-headed as they were swung around on the carousel. She had seen these things but had never ridden on one.

"This is so wonderful," Mandie called to Celia next to her.

"Yes, almost like riding my real horse back home," Celia agreed.

"I would prefer a real horse," Jonathan said from behind them. "If I had a real horse I could ride all over this park."

"And then gallop down to the wharf to the old boat," Mandie added with a smile as the breeze blew the curly wisps of blond hair around her face. She tightened her bonnet with one hand as she looked back at Jonathan.

"That's right," the boy agreed with a grin.

As Mandie turned to look forward again she glimpsed a short dark man standing by a fish pond nearby as the carousel spun around.

"Look!" she cried to her friends. "That man over there! He looks like the man we saw with the painting in the hotel."

As Jonathan and Celia quickly looked in the direction Mandie pointed as they swung past the pond again, the man looked directly at them and started hurrying down a nearby pathway.

"Oh, this thing has got to stop so we can go after him!" Mandie said excitedly, twisting to watch the man.

Just then it was time for the carousel to slow down and discharge its passengers. The three young people didn't wait for it to completely stop but jumped off on the last round. They stumbled and held on to each other to keep from falling as they straightened up and looked for the man.

"He's way down that path," Mandie said, rushing forward.

Her friends followed but the man was too quick for them. He glanced back and then darted into a side path and disappeared. The three searched every lane but could not find him.

"That man sure does know how to get away fast," Mandie said disappointedly as the three gave up their search.

"Mandie, he might not have been the same man from the hotel," Celia said.

"I think he was," Mandie replied. "He looked guilty, like he was trying to avoid us."

"He could have just been in a hurry. I'm not sure he was the same man either," Jonathan agreed with Celia as they started back up the pathway toward the carousel.

"Well, I think he was and sooner or later I'm going to catch up with him and prove it," Mandie said.

"Right now I'd be more interested in going back to the old boat," Jonathan said as they walked along.

Celia spoke up. "If y'all insist on going back to that boat tonight, you know all you have to do is lose interest in this park so Mrs. Taft and Senator Morton will decide to go back to the hotel."

Mandie stopped to look at her friend. "Celia, you're right. We'll just go over there and sit down with them." She smiled.

Jonathan grinned. "It's better to do that and get back early enough so we don't have to go to the boat in the dark."

"I don't think it would be safe to go down there on the wharf after dark," Celia warned her friends.

"All right, let's hurry up," Mandie replied as she walked ahead toward her grandmother and Senator Morton. "Maybe we can get to the boat soon after we go back to the hotel. Let's hurry."

Chapter 5 / Chased Away From the Boat

"Well, are y'all bored already with this beautiful park?" Mrs. Taft asked as the three young people sat down on a bench opposite her and Senator Morton.

"Not really. It's so big and you had asked us to stay within your sight so we have been through everything near here," Mandie replied as she realized she really was telling the truth. She and her friends had covered every inch within the vicinity of the adults.

"I'm just too worn out to walk around farther into the park, so why don't we just head back to the hotel for the night? I could use a cup of tea when we get there," Mrs. Taft said to Senator Morton.

"Why, yes, that would be fine," the man replied, standing up to give Mrs. Taft a hand as she also rose.

Mandie and her friends looked at one another. Tea! There goes our chance to get back to the boat tonight. *Grandmother will probably linger an hour over a cup of tea,* Mandie was thinking.

The three young people followed the adults out of the park and back up the avenue to the hotel. They didn't have a chance to talk, but they mouthed words at one another and made gestures while watching to see if Mrs. Taft and Senator Morton looked back at them.

Mandie sighed as she rolled her eyes at Jonathan and Celia and mouthed the word *tea*.

"Later," mouthed Jonathan. He made gestures, and silently added, "We go later."

Celia, watching the two, added her own silent comment. She shook her head and mouthed the words, "Too late. Dark."

Mandie shook her head and mouthed, "Maybe not. We'll be in a hurry to go up to our rooms."

Celia raised her eyebrows and Jonathan shrugged. Mrs. Taft looked back just then to be sure they were following.

Mandie pretended not to notice her grandmother's glance as she turned her attention to shopwindows along the way. She wasn't really seeing the merchandise displayed. She was trying to figure out in her mind just how they could reach the rope she was sure she had seen on the boat. There had to be a way to get aboard the vessel and she was going to find it.

When they reached the hotel, Mrs. Taft led everyone into the tea parlor where there were groupings of settees and chairs and where one could be served tea.

"I'm not much for tea," Mandie told her grandmother. "I'd rather have coffee if they have any." A waiter stood by.

"Yes, well, I miss my coffee back home, too. I doubt that they have American coffee like we're used to but I'll take a chance. How about you, Celia, and Jonathan?" Mrs. Taft asked.

"I'd love to have coffee," Celia said.

"Coffee is just what I need," Jonathan told her.

"Then I will make it unanimous," Senator Morton joined in. He gave the waiter the order.

Jonathan laughed and said, "That sort of sounds like politics, Senator. Is that the way they do things in Washington?"

"I'll have to admit sometimes the last voters go along with the majority on an issue," Senator Morton said with a silent laugh. "However, most of the time the senators are very set in their opinions. Senator Taft, Mrs. Taft's late husband here, was usually the leader in initiating decisions. He was a powerful man and he was well liked."

"Thank you, Senator," Mrs. Taft murmured.

"I wish I could have known my grandfather," Mandie said sadly.

"He probably died before you were born, Miss Amanda," the senator said, then turned to Mrs. Taft. "Isn't that right?"

"Not long after Amanda was born," Mrs. Taft said, and glancing at Mandie, added, "So you wouldn't have remembered him anyway if you had lived with us."

Mandie instantly cringed within herself. She was afraid Mrs. Taft would make some remark about her father again.

Celia spoke up with a statement that shocked everyone. "I think I'd like to be a senator someday."

Mandie and Jonathan laughed. Mrs. Taft smiled and Senator Morton said, "By the time you are old enough, who knows, we might have lady senators, but right now you'd better be concentrating on any studies that would help you later just in case."

Mandie couldn't imagine Celia as a senator. She was too meek and quiet. "You'd also better learn how to talk ninety miles an hour because you'd have to campaign and talk and talk and talk," Mandie teased.

Celia blushed as she protested, "Mandie, I know how to talk. I may not talk a whole lot like you do, but people usually listen to what I do say. There!" She tossed her head in the air.

"Celia, I was only teasing," Mandie said. "I'm sorry if I said the wrong thing. But you can laugh at me because I just might decide to become a writer."

"A writer? Oh, Mandie, you'd be a great writer!" Celia exclaimed.

"Yes, especially a writer of mysteries," Jonathan added with his mischievous grin.

"You're never too young to begin, Miss Amanda, and if that's what you want to do, I'd suggest you begin immediately keeping up with the journal I gave you to record this journey to Europe," Senator Morton told her seriously.

Mandie smiled at him and said, "I write in it now and then, but I promise to try harder to find the time to keep it current."

Mrs. Taft had listened to the conversation and now she spoke to Jonathan. "Since we're all deciding on our future careers, what are you interested in, Jonathan?"

Jonathan shrugged his shoulders, smiled at her and said, "I have no idea." He paused and then added, "Maybe I'd be good at being a detective."

The girls laughed then and he grinned at them. Mrs. Taft smiled and turned to talk to Senator Morton.

"Oh no!" Mandie exclaimed.

"Oh yes," Jonathan insisted. "I'll do the detective work and you can write stories about me." He grinned mischievously.

"All right, that's a bargain," Mandie agreed, and as

Mrs. Taft and Senator Morton carried on their own conversation, she bent close to his ear and added, "Like falling in the water at the pier!"

"Just don't forget to write about how you fell in the water, too, at the lake in Germany. Time-about is fair enough," Jonathan replied.

The waiter returned then with their coffee and some tiny rolls to go with it. As he placed everything on the table before them, Mrs. Taft sighed and said, "Oh, dear, I don't believe I could eat a bite, even though the rolls do look awfully delectable."

"I think I might be able to eat one or two after all that walking," Jonathan said with a grin.

"And I'll have a couple," Mandie said, helping herself.

Then as the adults continued their own conversation, Mandie quickly wrapped her rolls in her napkin and stuffed them in her purse. As Jonathan and Celia watched questioningly, she whispered, "For later. We may need some extra energy later."

At that moment Mrs. Taft turned to look at the young people and almost saw Mandie putting the rolls away. She looked at Mandie's empty plate and frowned and continued her conversation with the senator.

"Whew!" Jonathan whispered softly. "Almost caught." Then he helped himself to two more rolls and said loudly, "I'll just take these to give to Snowball, Mandie."

Mrs. Taft heard what he said and turned to look at him, but she went right on talking to the senator.

"Snowball? He's eaten so much since we've been in Europe I'm probably going to have to change his name to Butterball when we get home," Mandie said, laughing. She noticed her grandmother and the senator had both finished their coffee. "Grandmother, could Celia and I go on up to our rooms so I can give these rolls to Snowball?" she asked as Jonathan handed her his two rolls.

"I suppose so. You young people should get plenty of rest tonight," Mrs. Taft replied. "We've had a busy day today and tomorrow may be even busier."

"Thank you, Grandmother," Mandie said as she and friends stood up from the table.

"I feel like having more coffee. What about you, Senator?" Mrs. Taft asked.

"I was going to suggest that very thing," Senator Morton replied, turning to look about for the waiter.

"Good-night then, Grandmother, Senator Morton," Mandie said as she left the table. Celia and Jonathan joined her and after good-nights were exchanged, the young people hurried for the stairs to go to their rooms.

When they reached the first landing they stopped to talk.

"I wonder how long your grandmother and the senator will stay downstairs," Jonathan said.

"I don't know, but the tea parlor where they are is not near the front door so we can very easily slip out without them seeing us," Mandie said.

"What if your grandmother decides to stop by our rooms when she does come upstairs and we aren't there?" Celia asked.

"I don't think she will. Besides, if we hurry we may be able to get down to the old boat and back again before they even go to their rooms," Mandie replied.

"Thank goodness I closed the door to my bedroom when I left tonight since I share the suite with Senator Morton," Jonathan remarked.

"Then let's go. No use to go to our rooms and then come back," Mandie told her friends as she turned back down the stairs. "I'm sure when my grandmother does go upstairs she'll ride the elevator, which happens to be clear down at the other end of the hall. Come on."

Mandie led the way and they were able to slip out the front door without the manager seeing them. The gaslights on the street had already been lit. Lots of people were out for a stroll.

The three hurried down to the wharf and toward the old boat. Mandie was disappointed to find there were no streetlights near it. They carefully made their way in the dusky darkness out to the end of the pier.

"Oh, shucks, I can't see a thing!" Mandie exclaimed as she gazed at the outline of the old boat. "I can't tell whether there's a rope on it or not, can y'all?"

"No, I couldn't say either way," Jonathan said.

"Well, I have cat eyes. I can see something hanging on the side of the boat I think," Celia said, staring with her green eyes.

"But it's so dark we'd never be able to accomplish anything," Mandie complained. "All this trouble for nothing."

At that moment the moaning sound came from the old boat. It was louder than what they had heard before. In the darkness Mandie felt shivers run up and down her spine. Celia grasped Mandie's hand.

"W . . . we might as w-well go," Mandie decided and quickly walked back down the pier. Celia held tightly to her hand and Jonathan lost no time in following.

The three silently hurried away from the wharf until they reached the street with lights. Then they paused to get their breath. People were still walking around.

"We have to go back to the hotel now, but at the first crack of dawn we'll come back," Mandie told her friends. "All right with y'all?" She looked at Jonathan and Celia.

"I'll be ready," Jonathan promised.

"I suppose so," Celia hesitantly agreed.

The three young people slipped back into the hotel and up to their rooms without encountering anyone. They agreed to meet at the top of the stairs as soon as the sky lightened the next morning. Mandie gave Snowball the rolls. He ate Jonathan's and also the ones Mandie had taken. He was always hungry.

And to Mandie it seemed she had only dropped off to sleep when the light of day streaming in through the window by her bed woke her. She hastily sat up, rubbed her eyes, and jumped out of bed.

"Celia," she called to her friend who was still sleeping. "Are you going with Jonathan and me down to the old boat?"

"Mmmm," Celia grunted as she opened her eyes and sat up. "Of course."

She slid off the high bed and hurried to dress as Mandie pulled her dress on. Snowball, curled up on the foot of Mandie's bed, stood up and stretched and then decided to lie back down and sleep a little longer.

"Sorry, Snowball," Mandie told her cat as she picked him up. "I have to shut you in the bathroom so you can't get out. I'll put a nice soft pillow in there for you." She took a pillow from her bed, laid Snowball on it in the bathroom, and closed the door.

"We probably need a shawl, Mandie. I think it's cool this morning," Celia told her as she took a shawl from the bureau drawer and draped it around herself.

"Right," Mandie agreed as she did the same.

The girls hastily tied on their bonnets and slipped out of the room. The hallway was empty. There was no sign of anyone stirring around this early in the morning. They softly hurried to the top of the stairs and found Jonathan sitting on the steps waiting for them.

"Let's go," Mandie whispered to her friends.

They quietly rushed down the stairs. There was no one in sight at the front desk and they were able to get outside on the sidewalk without being seen.

"Now," Mandie exclaimed. "We made it!"

The three hurriedly made their way down to the old boat. There were very few people on the streets. The sun was just beginning to peep over the horizon.

Rushing ahead out onto the pier Mandie quickly surveyed the old boat and exclaimed, "I was right! There is a rope hanging over the side. Look!" She pointed.

"But I don't see how we can reach that," Celia said.

"And if we are able to reach it, we may find that it is loose and not even anchored to anything on the boat," Jonathan said.

"Well, we won't know until we find out," Mandie said, quickly looking about the pier. There was more of the old timber lying around and she searched for a long stick. "We need something to poke at it."

Jonathan and Celia helped search for a piece of timber long enough to reach to the boat. "Here!" Jonathan said, quickly pulling a long pole out from the bottom of a pile nearby. "See how long this is."

"Perfect," Mandie said as she helped.

They dragged the pole to the end of the pier and found it would reach the boat, but it was heavy and not flexible.

"I have an idea," Mandie suggested. "If we lie down on our stomachs on the floor on the pier and push the pole across to the boat, I think we can manage it."

"We can try," Jonathan said.

He and Mandie stretched out on the pier and shoved the pole at the boat while Celia watched. After several tries they were able to catch a loop of the rope with the pole. Then by twisting the pole and causing the rope to wrap around it, they were able to draw the rope toward the pier.

"Here it comes!" Mandie exclaimed as they withdrew the pole and the rope came with it.

When the pole finally cleared the edge of the pier, Mandie and Jonathan stood up and pulled on the rope. It seemed to be fastened to the boat at the other end.

"All right, it's secured to the boat somehow," Jonathan said.

"And all we have to do is fasten it real good and tight to the pier and then we can use it to swing on to get to the boat," Mandie said, looking around for something to hook it to.

"Swing on that rope over the water? Mandie, you can't swim, remember?" Celia told her.

"I know but I'm not going to fall in," Mandie replied as Jonathan helped her wrap the rope around a low post standing up from the floor of the pier. "I've swung on ropes before. Nothing to it."

"I'll go first so I can help you get over the side of the boat," Jonathan offered as he tested the strength of the rope.

"Please be careful," Mandie cautioned him.

The girls watched as Jonathan stooped, reached out with both hands, and grasped the rope beyond the edge of the pier. He swung down on it and began moving one hand after the other as he went toward the boat. Finally he made it and was able to climb over the side of the old boat. He stood there grinning.

"All right, watch out for me," Mandie told him as she followed what he had done. Just as she stepped off the pier and found herself swinging on the rope over the water, she became dizzy-headed and a little frightened.

She took several deep breaths, ignored the water beneath, and looked forward to where Jonathan was waiting.

Jonathan helped Mandie onto the boat and the two quietly crept toward the small cabin. Just as they got near the cracked window an ear-splitting moan burst through the air. They grasped each other in fright and stopped in their tracks. They waited for a minute or two but there was no more sound. Finally they got the nerve to creep closer and peek through the dirty window.

"I can't see much," Mandie said. "It's dark in there and this window is awfully dirty." She put her hands around her eyes, trying to see inside.

"Let me wipe some of that dirt off," Jonathan whispered as he took a large handkerchief from his pocket and vigorously rubbed at the glass. Now they could see better.

Suddenly another loud moan ripped through the air. The two drew quickly back and then when the sound died they peered inside.

"Look!" Mandie whispered. "There's a man on a cot in there and he seems to be crying."

"Yes," Jonathan agreed, wiping the glass again with his handkerchief.

To their amazement the man inside burst into sobs as they watched. He seemed to be crying his heart out about something.

"The poor man! There's something wrong with him," Mandie said softly as she and Jonathan pressed their noses against the glass to see inside.

And at that moment the man looked directly at them through the window. He jumped to his feet and came rushing out of the cabin door. He seemed to be wild as he waved his hands at them and yelled in English with a strange accent, "Go 'way! Get off my boat! Begone!" He looked like a giant. A thick reddish beard covered most of his face.

Mandie and Jonathan quickly slid over the side of the boat and onto the rope without even thinking whether the rope was strong enough to hold both of them at one time. They managed to get back to the pier and collapsed on the wooden floor as they surveyed the old boat.

Celia, who had stayed on the pier, came hovering over them and asked, "Are y'all all right?"

Mandie ignored her friend but watched as the man wiped his eyes with a dirty, ragged sleeve and went back inside the cabin.

"That man seems to be deranged," Jonathan commented as he stood up and dusted off his clothes.

"There's something wrong with him. I've never seen a big man cry like that before," Mandie said as she stood up and straightened her skirt.

"He didn't even notice the rope. Evidently he only wanted us off his boat," Jonathan said.

"Maybe we'd better untie it on this end and wrap it around a post under the pier where no one will notice it," Mandie said as she walked toward the tied end of the rope.

"Hadn't you just better untie and drop it loose?" Celia asked, and then when Mandie didn't answer, she said, "Y'all are not planning on going over there again?"

Mandie smiled at her and said, "Sure. I want to know who that man is and why he is crying."

"And why he's on a dilapidated boat like that," Jonathan added.

Celia sighed and shrugged her shoulders.

"After all, that man may need some help," Mandie added as she and Jonathan tied the end of the rope under the pier while they lay on their stomachs.

She stood up and shook out her skirt. "Right now we need to get back to the hotel and change our clothes for breakfast before we are missed. But I do plan to come back."

Chapter 6 / More Investigations

The three hurried back to the hotel and up to their rooms without taking time to discuss their discovery. That could be done later, Mandie decided. Right now they had to get dressed by the time Mrs. Taft and Senator Morton were ready for breakfast.

Mandie and Celia quickly bathed and dressed while Snowball roamed their rooms. Hurriedly taking down a white voile dress with rose sprigs scattered over it, Mandie slipped into it and then combed and brushed her long blond hair. Back home she usually wore it in one long plait down the back, but while she was in Europe she liked to let it hang loose, tied back with a ribbon. That made her feel grown-up. Today she secured it with a white headband over which her matching bonnet would comfortably fit later.

Celia, already clad in a bright yellow dress, watched her friend as Mandie twirled before the mirror.

"You look beautiful, Mandie," Celia told her.

Mandie immediately stood still and looked at Celia. "And you look more beautiful than that. Too bad Tommy and Robert aren't here, huh?"

"It would be nice to have them along once in a while," Celia replied as she hung a strand of pearls around her neck.

Tommy Patton and Robert Rogers attended Mr. Chadwick's School for Boys in Asheville, North Carolina, near the girl's school. They had become good friends during the past school year and it had turned out that Tommy's parents were friends of Mandie's mother.

Mandie sighed and said, "But it would be interesting to have Joe Woodard see us dressed in all the finery we've been wearing here in Europe." She laughed and added, "He probably wouldn't approve."

"Oh, he wouldn't approve of Jonathan, that's for sure," Celia teased as she twirled before the mirror.

"No, Joe is just a good old country boy back in Charley Gap and Jonathan is a man of the world. They wouldn't understand each other at all," Mandie agreed as she sat on a nearby chair. "I'll really be glad to get back home among my own kind of people. This has been an interesting journey but I wouldn't want to do it again."

"Oh, Mandie, remember your grandmother mentioned sending you to Europe to school?" Celia said anxiously as she sat in another chair. "You may have to come back and live here, at least for school."

"No, I won't do it!" Mandie said emphatically as she rose from the chair. "I told Grandmother I didn't want to do that and I mean it. I don't think my mother will make me do it. It would be too far away from her. I wouldn't even have time to come home for holidays, it takes so long to get over here." She sat back down.

"Well, I wouldn't want to attend school over here either," Celia agreed. "And I am sure my mother would never even suggest such a thing. Why, I'd think she didn't love me if she wanted to send me so far away."

Snowball tried to jump into Mandie's lap. She put her hand out to stop him. "You'll wrinkle my dress before I even get started today, Snowball." He sat on the floor and meowed at her.

Mandie reached down to rub Snowball's head. "I know I've neglected you lately, but I promise to take you out today," she told him. "If Grandmother doesn't want you along wherever she's taking us today, then I'll let you go with us when we go back to the old boat. But you will have to promise not to try to jump into the fishing boats again." Snowball meowed loudly.

"When are you planning to go back to the old boat?" Celia asked.

Mandie straightened up and looked at her friend. "I don't know. Just whenever I can get a chance. I wonder what's wrong with that man on the boat. He sounded awfully heartbroken or something, but he was so big I was afraid of him when he started yelling at Jonathan and me."

"I know. I was glad I had stayed on the pier," Celia agreed. "Mandie, I wonder if we'll ever see that other man again, the one you think stole the painting?"

"I hope so," Mandie replied. "I want to find out for sure whether he is the thief. I'd just love to be able to go back and tell that rude guard at the museum that I had caught the man who stole the painting."

"The rude guard? Oh, that guard who told you not to touch the muslin hanging over the blank space where the painting had been," Celia replied.

"Yes. I don't think I was doing anything wrong, but he caused that argument between my grandmother and me and I don't think she's forgiven me yet," Mandie said.

"Have you forgiven her for whatever she said that made you angry?" Celia asked, looking closely at her friend.

Mandie jumped up and walked around the room. "You don't know what happened because I haven't told you," she said. There was a knock at the door. "And that must be Grandmother now."

Mandie crossed the room and opened the door to find Jonathan standing there. "Oh, I thought you were my grandmother," she said.

"Not hardly," Jonathan said with a big grin. "She sent me after you girls. She and Senator Morton have just gone down the elevator."

Mandie was surprised that her grandmother had not let her know they were ready. "Well, I wonder why she didn't wait for us," she said. Turning back to Celia, she called, "Come on. Grandmother has already gone downstairs."

The three hurried down the stairs and arrived in the lobby just as the elevator with Mrs. Taft and Senator Morton got to the main floor. Greetings were exchanged and the adults led the way into the dining room.

After they were all seated, Mrs. Taft and the senator talked and completely ignored the young people until the waiter came to take their order for breakfast. That gave Mandie and her friends a chance to discuss in low tones their morning escapade.

"When do you want to go back to the boat?" Jonathan whispered to the girls.

"Soon as possible," Mandie replied under her breath. Leaning close to Jonathan she asked, "Are you afraid of that big man?"

Jonathan grinned, shook his head, and said, "Of course not. Are you?"

"He's awfully big and fierce," Mandie replied softly. "But we need to find out what's wrong with him. Maybe we could help."

"He could be dangerous, Mandie," Celia whispered.

At that moment the waiter appeared and Mrs. Taft asked what they wanted for breakfast. The young people had found that eggs tasted pretty much the same in all the countries in Europe as they did back home so the order was unanimous for eggs and hot rolls.

When the waiter left, Mrs. Taft told the young people, "Senator Morton and I are going to a reception this morning. I understand there is to be a continuous music presentation in the main drawing room across the hall there, so you all can attend that while we're gone."

Mandie and her friends silently looked at one another.

Senator Morton added, "We should return shortly after the noon meal."

"What kind of music is this going to be?" Mandie asked.

"I believe it will vary from magicians to operatic," the senator explained as Mrs. Taft looked at him.

"What are we supposed to do about eating at noon?" Jonathan asked.

Mrs. Taft smiled at him and said, "Y'all just eat right here and sign the ticket. The manager will put it on our bill."

Mandie was not too happy about having to attend this "music presentation," as her grandmother called it, but at least they didn't have to go dragging around all day sightseeing. All she really wanted to do was return to the old boat. Maybe the show would end before her grandmother and the senator returned, and she and her friends would have time to go to the wharf again.

As soon as the meal was finished Mrs. Taft and Senator Morton rose.

"It's time for us to get going," Mrs. Taft told the young people. "Y'all have about thirty minutes before time for the show, so you can either sit here or go to your rooms till then. If y'all will eat about noontime, then you should be finished by the time we get back. We'll all do a little sightseeing afterward."

"Yes, Grandmother," Mandie said as she and her friends stayed at the table.

"Our carriage should be waiting by now," Senator Morton told Mrs. Taft as they hurriedly left the room.

Mandie watched them out of sight, then turned to her friends, smiled and said, "What a great idea Grandmother had today!"

"You call sitting through a boring music show a great idea?" Jonathan asked.

"But there's always intermission at these doings; in fact, several intermissions in some shows," Mandie reminded him. "And sometimes they're long enough that we could run down to the old boat and back."

"Mandie! You wouldn't!" Celia exclaimed.

"I very carefully noticed that my grandmother never said one word about not leaving the hotel," Mandie replied.

"And as long as we attend the show, we can do whatever we want during intermissions," Jonathan added.

"Oh, well!" Celia sighed as she looked at her two friends.

Mandie quickly stood up from the table. "Come on, let's get our bonnets. And I need something to eat for Snowball." She hurriedly dumped scraps from their plates onto a linen napkin and rolled it up.

Jonathan went up the steps with the girls as far as the landing and then told them, "I'll wait right here for you. Don't be too long."

"We'll hurry," Mandie said as she and Celia rushed down the corridor to their rooms.

Snowball met them at the door with a loud meow. Mandie had forgotten to shut him in the bathroom when she left earlier. The maid had made the beds but hadn't let the cat escape.

"Thank goodness you're still here," Mandie told him as she put the scraps on his plate in the bathroom. He quickly began devouring the food.

Mandie and Celia picked up their bonnets and put them on.

"I'm going to have to take Snowball with me. He hasn't been outside in so long," Mandie said, reaching for his red leash and harness on the bureau.

"Do you mean in the drawing room with us, Mandie?" Celia asked.

"I guess I'll have to," Mandie said as she stooped and fastened the harness on her cat, who was now licking his paws. "If he misbehaves I can take him out."

Mandie picked up her kitten and the girls rejoined Jonathan on the landing. By the time they got downstairs, the drawing room was filling up with a variety of people to see the show. The young people took seats on the back row near the door.

"We can get out faster from back here," Mandie told her friends. "Besides, I may have to take Snowball out if he doesn't want to sit in my lap."

Snowball stood up in Mandie's lap and looked around the room. When the music started he finally curled up to sleep. Mandie kept her hand on his back to be sure he didn't suddenly jump down and run off.

The three young people became so interested in the magician's tricks during the first part of the show they were surprised when intermission was announced.

"Please return in thirty minutes, ladies and gentlemen," the man on the stage was saying. "You will find tea in the parlor."

"Thirty minutes! Let's hurry!" Mandie said, quickly jumping up. They dashed out the doorway ahead of the crowd and on outside to the avenue.

They raced down the street to the wharf and to the old boat, ignoring the stares of passersby. Mandie carried Snowball with one arm and held up her long skirt with the other.

Finally standing on the pier, they looked at the old boat. Mandie asked Celia to hold Snowball while she and Jonathan pulled the rope out from under the floor where they had hidden it. They quickly straightened it out and tied it around the post on the pier.

"Are you coming with us this time?" Mandie asked Celia.

"No, maybe later. I'll just stay here and hold Snowball for you," Celia said.

"Thanks," Mandie replied.

Jonathan went first across the rope to the old boat and Mandie followed. They quietly stepped over the side of the boat and crept up to the window of the cabin. The man was still lying on the bunk inside and he looked as though he might be asleep.

Mandie and Jonathan stepped back from the window and whispered to each other.

"What should we do now?" Mandie asked in a soft voice.

"I don't think we ought to wake him up," Jonathan replied in a hushed voice. "He would be awfully mean if we did."

Suddenly there was a noise at the side of the boat. Mandie slipped far enough around the corner of the cabin to look. She jumped back and told Jonathan, "Someone is coming!"

Together they slid behind some old cans and timber and watched. A short dark man was climbing on board from a rope ladder hanging over the side. As they held their breath and looked, the man pushed open the door to the cabin and went inside. He was carrying a large package, which he placed on a shelf near the bed.

Mandie stood up enough to try to see better, but she was afraid she would be seen so she darted back down.

"You have to leave this boat, Alex," they heard the man say in British English.

Then the big man yelled at the other man, "Get off my boat!"

The short man yelled back at Alex, "You can't solve any problems holing up on this broken-down boat. Come with me."

"I cannot leave this boat and you know it," Alex loudly told him. "I am guilty!"

"You are not guilty," the other man tried to convince him. "Come with me."

"I know that I am guilty," Alex insisted. "And you know it, too. Now get off my boat and don't come back!"

"All right, Alex. I will go but I will come back," the other man said.

Mandie and Jonathan shrank behind the trash pile as the dark man came out of the cabin. Mandie got a good look at him then as he used the rope ladder to go down the side of the boat.

"He's the man who had the painting!" Mandie whispered excitedly in Jonathan's ear.

Jonathan looked but didn't reply.

As soon as the man was out of sight, the two ran to see how he had managed to come up by the rope ladder.

They looked down and saw him stepping off the ladder that was hanging from the floor of the pier. He quickly walked away down the walkway.

Mandie suddenly realized Celia was nowhere in sight. "Where is Celia?" she exclaimed. "I don't see her!"

"Let's go see," Jonathan said, leading the way to the rope ladder.

The two followed what the man had done and came up on the pier. Mandie straightened up and looked around. Then she saw Celia way down another walkway that branched off from the main pier. Mandie waved to her and Celia, carrying Snowball, hurried toward them.

"Did you see that man?" Mandie quickly asked Celia as she caught up with her and Jonathan.

"Yes, I did. That's why I went way down there. I didn't know who he was, and there I was all alone on the pier, so I picked up Snowball and walked away," Celia explained as she handed the kitten to Mandie.

"I'm pretty sure he's the man we saw in the hotel with the painting," Mandie told her. She related the conversation that she and Jonathan had overheard between the two men. "The man on the boat is guilty of something, so they must both be crooks of some kind."

"I sure am glad I walked away from him, then," Celia said, with a gasp.

"Which way did he go? Did you notice?" Mandie asked as she looked around.

"No. I didn't want to look at him or draw his attention," Celia said.

"I know which way we'd better go," Jonathan said. "Intermission is probably over by now."

"I hope not!" Mandie exclaimed as she held on to Snowball and they all hurried back toward the hotel.

As they reached the drawing room door, the music

began and they were lucky enough to find their seats on the back row empty. Mandie put Snowball in her lap as they sat down.

An orchestra on the stage was playing awfully loud music. Mandie, sitting on the end of the row, had leaned across Celia to whisper to Jonathan when she suddenly caught sight of a short dark man at the far end of the row in front of them. He looked like the man who had been at the boat from what she could see of the back of his head. But how could that be? Would that man leave the old boat and then come up here to the hotel and sit down for a concert?

She whispered to her friends and motioned for them to look at the man. "Is that the man we saw on the boat?"

Jonathan and Celia both stared at the back of the man's head. Jonathan shrugged his shoulders and mouthed, "I don't know."

Celia shook her head.

Mandie couldn't decide, but she continued to watch the man in case he turned around enough to see him full in the face.

Snowball didn't like the loud music and wanted to move around in his mistress' lap. When Mandie gave him a pat to sit still, he suddenly jumped down to the floor. Mandie quickly pulled on his leash. This time he didn't manage to escape. She bent and picked him up and held him tight.

Then she remembered the man. She looked down the row and found he was gone. She glanced through the crowd and couldn't see him. How did he get out of the room so fast? And why did he leave? Where did he go?

Mandie was furious with Snowball for causing her to lose sight of the man. There was no telling where he had gone.

Chapter 7 / Trouble!

As Mandie gazed about the room in search of the man who had been sitting at the far end of the row in front of her and her friends, the man on the stage was concluding the concert.

"Ladies and gentlemen, due to the indisposition of Aurelia, our soprano who was supposed to perform next, we are obliged to close the performance," the man told the audience. "Because of an acute sore throat, Aurelia is unable to sing a note, but we hope she will be able to appear later this week. Thank you for coming. We appreciate your patronage."

"Well, that leaves us free for a good long while before Grandmother and Senator Morton get back," Mandie said to her friends as they all stood up.

"And I know how you want to spend the time," Jonathan teased as they turned to leave the room.

Mandie smiled at him. "I'd like to walk around and look for that man who was sitting down the row. He just

89

evaporated really. He was there one moment and the next he was gone."

"I didn't see him get up and leave," Celia said as the three walked over to one side of the corridor to watch the audience coming out of the concert.

"Neither did I," Jonathan said. "He certainly was fast, whatever way he went."

"You see, that sounds like a thief. A thief would have to be fast," Mandie told her friends. "So no one would notice him."

"Or her," Jonathan said, grinning. "No one knows whether the thief of that painting was a man or a woman because no one was there when it happened."

"You're right," Celia agreed. "There are women thieves same as men."

While they were talking they were watching the people mill about in the corridor. Mandie held Snowball in her arms.

"I suppose by the size of the painting and the height that it was hung, a woman could have stolen it. But I think it was a man, and I believe it was the one we saw here in the hotel," Mandie insisted. "And I am going to keep looking until I find him."

At that moment the manager came walking down the hallway, and when he saw Mandie and her friends, he stopped to speak to Jonathan.

"We were able to do an excellent cleaning of your wet clothes, and the maid has hung them in your wardrobe," the tall gray-haired man said. His English had an accent. "We have a wire message at the desk for your Honorable Morton. We would be pleased you tell him."

"A message for Senator Morton?" Jonathan questioned excitedly. "Sir, could I possibly see the message? Senator Morton will not return until after the noon meal, and the message may be urgent."

"Of course. Follow me please," the manager said, leading the way up the corridor and to the front reception room where the desk clerk was stationed.

The manager went behind the desk as the clerk looked at the young people. He took a paper from a pigeonhole and handed it to Jonathan. "Here is the message to which I refer."

Jonathan took the paper, unfolded it, and read aloud: " 'Would be delighted to have Jonathan visit with us. However, we arrived home today and will be going on another assignment tomorrow. Please keep us in touch with your travel locations. Will inform you as soon as we know when we will be home to receive Jonathan. Soon we think. . . .' And it's signed by my aunt." He checked the paper over and then glanced at his friends.

"Oh, Jonathan, it looks like you will be able to visit your aunt and uncle in Paris after all," Mandie said excitedly.

During their European travels Senator Morton had tried to contact Jonathan's relatives where the boy wanted to stay for a while. His father was always away somewhere tending to his vast business, and was always leaving Jonathan in boarding schools in various countries. Jonathan was tired of all this and was hoping his father would permit him to stay in Paris with the aunt and uncle who worked for a branch of an American newspaper.

"Don't celebrate yet," Jonathan said, frowning. "My father has to give permission, remember? And Senator Morton hasn't heard from him yet."

"I think your father will allow you to stay with your relatives, Jonathan," Celia said.

"If we can get a chance we'll talk him into it," Mandie said, laughing. And then she looked at the boy and asked,

"Or would you rather go home to New York and live there, in your own house?"

Jonathan looked at the floor, shuffled his feet and replied, "If that could be possible. I mean, if my father would stay home instead of traveling all over the world all the time. But even then I'd still like to stay with my aunt and uncle until time for school to start. Then I could go home to New York."

The manager had stood behind the counter, watching and listening and now he said, "If you please. I must hold the message for your Honorable Morton."

"Oh yes, sir," Jonathan said, handing the paper back to the man. "Thank you for letting me read it."

The manager nodded, smiled, and said, "You will please inform your Honorable Morton that the message awaits him?"

"Yes, sir, I will," Jonathan told him.

The three walked across the huge room to stand by the front door as the crowd still moved about the hotel.

"Oh, I wish Uncle Ned would hurry up and get into town," Mandie said as she watched the people. "I thought he would have been here before now."

"You think he could help us find that man, don't you?" Jonathan asked.

"I know he could. After all, he's full-blooded Cherokee and the Cherokees are experts at finding people or things," Mandie said. "He always knows what to do when I get involved in something."

"Well, are we going to stand here and waste all that precious time we have before your grandmother and the senator come back?" Jonathan said, his lips turned up in a mischievous grin.

"I was thinking about that, but I haven't decided what we ought to do next," Mandie replied, holding on to

Snowball as he squirmed to get down. "We could go walk on the streets and watch out for that man with the painting, or we could go back down to the old boat where the bearded man is."

"The bearded man whose name is Alex. Remember the other man called him Alex?" Jonathan reminded her.

"He called him that, but if he's a criminal that may not be his real name," Mandie replied.

"And the man with the painting y'all talk about, he wouldn't still be carrying around a painting with him, I'm sure," Celia said.

"No. If he stole it he'd probably hide it somewhere," Mandie agreed. "But I know what he looks like."

"We look sorta dumb just standing here by the door. Why don't we go walk outside?" Jonathan suggested as various people looked at them as they passed by.

"And watch for that man," Mandie said, leading the way through the doorway into the street.

The three stopped outside to decide where to walk.

"We've been down to the wharf several times. Why don't we go the other way?" Jonathan suggested.

"No, no, no!" Mandie said excitedly, quickly walking toward the wharf. "There goes that man!" She pointed ahead through the crowd as she held on to Snowball and lifted her long skirt to hurry after the man.

Jonathan and Celia looked in the direction she pointed and hastened after her.

Mandie kept watching for a glimpse of the man as she hurried past the people strolling on the avenue. He was evidently in an awfully big hurry the way he was pushing between people. Jonathan got ahead of Mandie and called back to her and Celia, "Come on!"

"No, Jonathan! We don't want him to see us. We just want to see where he's going," Mandie told him as she grasped his coattail to slow him down.

"All right, why didn't you say so?" Jonathan said, pulling his coat from her hand as she came alongside him. Celia was close behind.

"And here you're going to be a detective!" Mandie teased. "If he sees us he'll disappear again."

The short dark man ahead that Mandie had decided was the one they had seen with the painting suddenly slowed his steps and began browsing in the shopwindows along the way.

"I wonder what changed his mind about hurrying," Mandie said to her friends as they stayed a short distance behind him.

As she spoke the man suddenly began almost running. He turned into a nearby alley. Mandie realized it was the same place they had lost him the day before. She called "Come on!" to her friends as she ran after him.

The three had almost caught up with him when he abruptly stopped, pushed open a door, and entered. The young people hesitated as they came to the door. It was impossible to see what lay inside.

Mandie immediately made a decision and turned to her friends. "I'm going inside." Before they could speak, she pushed open the door and rushed inside. Celia and Jonathan followed. There was no sound and no sign of anyone.

"It's so dark I can't see anything," Celia whispered. She reached for Mandie's hand.

"Hold on to me," Mandie said softly as she squeezed Celia's hand and made her way forward.

"I'll bring up the rear," Jonathan told the girls as he stayed right behind Celia.

They seemed to be in a stone passageway that went downhill. The air was chilly and smelled of fish. Snowball, in Mandie's arms, was trying his best to get down. Evidently the odor affected him.

The stone floor was full of holes and bumps and caused them to trip now and then. Mandie found it hard to keep looking ahead to see the man and at the same time watch where she was walking. Suddenly the tunnel curved and she fell on some steps as the floor lowered. The jolt freed Snowball and he ran off ahead of her.

"Are you hurt?" Jonathan asked as he helped Mandie get to her feet.

"No, but Snowball ran away," Mandie said, quickly brushing off her long skirt and hurrying on.

"Snowball, come back here. You hear me?" Mandie called after the kitten as he raced ahead.

There was light filtering into the passageway now from open grills high above on the walls. Mandie could see an opening in the distance and she knew Snowball would go through it. She held up her long skirts and ran faster. Jonathan and Celia stayed right behind her.

"Well, look at this?" Mandie exclaimed as she paused for a moment at the end of the passageway. They were outside on the wharf near the old boat. She saw Snowball racing out onto the pier. He could fall into the water.

"I'll get him," Jonathan called to her as he sprinted onto the wooden pier and managed to grasp Snowball by his tail. Snowball angrily turned on him and was about to scratch when Mandie got to them and stooped down to swat at the kitten.

"Don't you dare!" Mandie told the white kitten. She picked him up and scolded him. "Snowball, you cause so much trouble. I may have to leave you in the hotel from now on." Snowball meowed as though he understood but swished his tail in agitation.

Celia caught her breath and said, "I'll carry him part of the time, Mandie."

"Thanks. I'll hold on to him until he calms down," Mandie told her. "That man has disappeared again. He could have gone into any of the openings in the sides of the tunnel."

"Or he could have come out here and gone onto the boat," Jonathan reminded her.

The three stood looking at the old boat. There was no sign of anyone on it.

"Let's go on the boat and look around," Mandie told her friends. "We can at least see if that bearded man, Alex, is still there."

The three walked toward the edge where the rope ladder was swinging.

"I'll stay here and hold Snowball for you, Mandie," Celia offered.

"No. I'll take him with me because I want you to come with us," Mandie replied. "Some stranger may see you alone here on the pier and it could be dangerous."

Celia hesitated and then agreed, "Well, all right, but I hope I don't fall into the water."

"You won't if you'll just hold tight to the ladder," Jonathan said. "I'll go ahead and reach back for Snowball, Mandie, so you can have both your hands free," he added as he started down the ladder.

At the bottom he stopped, and Mandie handed the kitten down to him as she clung to the top.

"Come on, Celia," Mandie coaxed her friend as she looked back up at Celia. "I'll wait here for you."

Celia carefully descended the rope ladder and finally stood on the crossbar underneath with her friends. Jonathan then gave Snowball to Mandie until he was halfway up the other ladder on the side of the boat. He stretched back and took Snowball and shoved him over onto the deck of the vessel. The girls followed. Mandie watched

Celia in case she needed any help and saw that her friend had no problem at all with the ladders.

The three hurriedly crouched behind the trash pile on the deck and waited to see if anyone heard them.

"Let's look through the window," Mandie whispered as she began creeping toward the window in a lowered position. Her friends followed.

They cautiously peeked in the window and saw the man, Alex, lying on the bunk bed staring at the ceiling as great sobs came from his throat. Then he suddenly sat up on the side of the bed. The three quickly ducked down out of his sight. And when they did Mandie lost hold of Snowball, and he ran across the deck to the cabin door, which was slightly open.

Mandie sighed in anger as the kitten pushed through the crack and into the cabin. The young people raised up enough to watch through the window to see where Snowball went. The kitten walked over to Alex and rubbed around his ankles. Alex ignored him for a few moments; then he looked down at the white kitten and picked him up.

"Well, where did you come from?" he said. "Just like my baby's kitten, you are." He rubbed Snowball's fur and held him up against his bearded face.

Snowball evidently didn't like the rough beard and he wriggled until the man put him down. The kitten ran back outside on the deck and Mandie captured him. The three peeked through the window to see what the man was doing.

Alex shook his head and looked about the litter-strewn cabin. "Must have been a dream, that kitten, come back from the dead." He stretched out again on the bunk bed.

"We might as well go and look somewhere else for

that other man," Mandie whispered to her friends.

As the three started moving toward the ladder on the side of the boat, Mandie heard a noise. She gasped. "Quick! Someone is coming!"

The young people scrambled for cover behind the trash pile. They watched to see who was coming up the ladder. As a head appeared over the side, Mandie decided it was the man they'd been following. He was carrying a large bag.

He stepped over onto the deck and went directly to the cabin. The three crept near the window to look and eavesdrop. The man put the bag on a shelf near the bunk bed and spoke to Alex.

"Get up, Alex," he said, bending over him. "I want to talk to you."

"Go 'way!" Alex mumbled crossly.

"Alex, you have to stop this. And you have to leave this boat," the man insisted, standing there looking at Alex. "This has lasted long enough."

Alex jumped from the bed and stood towering above the other man. "I said go! And I be meaning that! This boat is my home and I won't be leaving it."

"But, Alex, you can't live like this—" the other man said.

Alex moved toward him. "I live like this if I want. Now go!" He shook his fist at the man.

The other man left so suddenly that he caught the three young people looking through the window as he came out onto the deck. Surprised, he paused to look at them, then simply said, "Poor fellow, he needs all the help he can get." He turned quickly and disappeared down the ladder.

Alex had followed the man outside, and when he saw the three young people, he waved his hands wildly in the air, shouting, "Go! Get off my boat! Go 'way!" He moved threateningly toward them.

Mandie pushed Celia to go first down the ladder and then she scrambled down after her by one hand as she held Snowball in the other arm. Jonathan was close behind her. The three stood on the crossbar below and caught their breath.

"Whew! That was close!" Jonathan said.

Mandie, glancing overhead, saw the man named Alex looking down at them.

"It's still close. Let's go!" She led the way up the other rope ladder and they all collapsed on the floor of the pier.

"You saw that other man close up," Jonathan said as they sat there. "Do you still think he was the same one we saw with the painting in the hotel?"

Mandie thought for a moment. "Well, yes, I believe he is. In fact, his voice even sounded the same."

"Mandie, almost all the people we've heard speaking English talked with an English accent and so did he," Celia said.

"Anyhow, I think he was the same man and now he has disappeared again," Mandie insisted. She stood up as she held tightly to Snowball and shook out her long skirts.

"What do you suggest next?" Jonathan asked as he and Celia also rose.

"I think we ought to go back through that tunnel and explore it for hidden doors and rooms or whatever, someplace where he could hide because he disappeared into that tunnel," Mandie replied.

"But if that was the same man we just saw here, he came to the boat," Celia said.

"But we got here first so he detoured somewhere," Mandie said. She began walking back off the pier and her friends followed. At the wharf she looked around. "Let's see now. The opening to that tunnel must be that way." She pointed to the left.

As the three hurried in that direction, Mandie realized she was right. This was the place they had come out of the passageway. She stopped to speak to her friends. "Now let's be extra quiet in case he is inside. And this time I have Snowball's leash wrapped around my wrist so he can't get away again."

The three quickly entered the tunnel and then paused to look around. This end was not as dark as the other one. They could see there were no exits in this part. Mandie moved slowly forward and Celia and Jonathan followed.

The light grew darker and darker as they walked along and examined the walls for a door or some kind of cross tunnel. Then they rounded the bend where Mandie had fallen on the steps.

"There's a door!" Mandie whispered to her friends as she pointed toward the right side of the wall.

The three paused to look it over. Then Mandie made up her mind. "Let's open it," she said. She reached forward and slowly pushed the door open. It swung wide on squeaky hinges. They could see a small room inside with another door at the far end. The room was empty.

"I don't think we ought to go any farther," Celia objected.

"Just one more door," Mandie insisted as she walked across the room. Jonathan helped her push on the door. He tried so hard he lost his footing and banged his head on the old wooden facing as the big heavy door swung open. He rubbed his forehead as he and the girls looked inside. The room was full of wooden boxes.

"Let's see what's in those boxes," Mandie said. She

walked over to a stack and her friends followed. As they crossed the room the old door swung shut, cutting off most of the light in the tiny room.

"I'll open it again," Jonathan said. He pushed at the door but couldn't get it to budge. Mandie and even Celia helped but they couldn't get it to open.

Mandie looked around the room. The only light in it was coming through grills high on the walls like the ones they had seen in the tunnel earlier. But there was no other door to the room.

"We just have to get that door open," Mandie insisted. She quickly tied Snowball's leash to a handle on one of the wooden boxes. Going over to the door she pushed with all her might. Jonathan and Celia helped. The door wouldn't move.

The three stood back looking at the door. Celia had a frightened look on her face and Jonathan shrugged. But Mandie was angry with the door. They just had to get that door open! There was no other way out. The door hadn't seemed all that tight when they opened it. Could someone have bolted it on the outside when it had swung shut? And what was in all those stacks and stacks of boxes? Whatever it was, maybe someone would come to get some of the boxes and they could get out.

Mandie was really frightened but she tried to ignore it. Then Celia looked at her and said, "Our verse, Mandie."

The three young people joined hands and repeated Mandie's favorite Bible verse: "What time I am afraid I will put my trust in Thee."

Mandie sighed and looked at her friends. "Now I feel better."

"So do I," Celia agreed.

Jonathan shrugged his shoulders and walked around the room. "We might as well start on these boxes and see what's in them."

"They look like they're securely bound with those metal bands. I'm not so sure we can get them open," Mandie replied as she bent to inspect the one Snowball was tied to.

"There's no telling what's in them," Celia said.

"We'll just find out," Mandie said.

Chapter 8 / The Underground

Mandie and her friends focused their attention on the stacks of boxes in the room. Jonathan picked up several and found they were all heavy.

"They probably all have the same thing inside, whatever it is," Mandie remarked as she, too, tried to lift a box.

"And whatever is inside is packed firmly because nothing shakes around or rattles inside when I shake them," Jonathan added as he kept pulling boxes down from the top of the stacks and lining them up on the floor.

"Why don't we drop one real hard and see what happens?" Celia suggested.

Mandie and Jonathan looked at her. "But, Celia," Mandie said, "there might be something fragile inside and it would break if we slammed the box down."

"But we might also get a box to pop open if we drop it enough, and then we could see what's inside," Celia insisted.

"You mean like this?" Jonathan said with his mischievous grin as he picked up a box, held it high, and then let it fall to the floor. It only made a loud thud and the box did not break open. He picked it up again and repeated this several times. Nothing happened.

"They're awfully strong boxes," Mandie remarked as she examined the one Jonathan had been dropping.

"Yes, and they're all alike, good thick wood, bound with metal bands," Jonathan added as he looked around the room.

Mandie suddenly gasped. "What is Snowball doing?" She ran to bend over the white kitten who was busy pulling straw out from between the cracks of the box he was tied to.

"Smart cat!" Jonathan exclaimed.

"This box is cracked down the side," Mandie commented as she watched her kitten steadily working on the straw. "If we just leave him alone long enough, he'll probably get enough of that straw out so we can see what's inside."

The three stood back and watched. Snowball looked up at his mistress and meowed as though he thought she was going to scold him. He quit clawing at the straw and began licking his paws.

Mandie bent down to pat him on the head. "Oh, Snowball, why don't you go ahead and get all that straw out?" She pulled at the strands sticking out through the crack in the box but it kept breaking off.

"Too bad we don't have sharp fingernails like Snowball's claws," Jonathan remarked as he tried to help.

Mandie suddenly stood up. "This box already has a crack in it," she said. "If all three of us stood on top of it, we might be able to split it open."

Her friends agreed. Mandie tied Snowball to another

box, and then they went to work. Since the box was not very large, they had to hold tightly to one another in order to have room to stand.

"Now when I say go, we will all jump up and down as hard as we can," Mandie told her friends. "Ready?"

Celia and Jonathan both said, "Yes."

"One, two, three, jump!" Mandie cried. The three jumped up and stomped heavily on the box. They paused to see if they had been able to accomplish anything. "The crack does look a little wider," Mandie told them as she bent to inspect it.

"Then let's do it again," Jonathan said.

They kept jumping up and down on the box with little results. Mandie finally bent and began pulling on the straw again. Her friends helped.

"This stuff is scratching my fingers," Mandie said, pausing to look at her hands.

"Mine, too," Celia said.

"What's a few scratches? Come on, let's get this done," Jonathan told the girls. Then he suddenly stuck a small splinter in his finger and jumped up, dancing around the room.

"And what's wrong with you?" Mandie asked.

"Here, get this out for me," he said, holding out his right forefinger. "See that splinter?"

Mandie looked. "It's awfully small," she said as she tried to grasp the end of it. She squeezed his finger, trying to remove the sliver, but it wouldn't come out. Then she had an idea. She stood up and unclasped the broach she was wearing.

"What are you doing?" Jonathan asked.

"I'm going to use the end of this pin on the broach to pick the splinter out," Mandie told him as she reached for his hand. Before he could object she stuck the pin under the broken skin and then yanked out the splinter.

Jonathan immediately put his finger in his mouth and sighed with relief. "That tiny little thing really stuck," he said.

Mandie held out the splinter to him. "Here, you have to put this in your hair so the place won't get sore or infected," she said.

Jonathan looked at her questioningly. "Put it in my hair? Then it will stick in my head," he said, refusing the splinter. "Where did you get such a wild idea?"

Mandie thought for a moment as she still extended the splinter to him. "I don't really know. I've heard that all my life. My father used to do that," she said. "I suppose it's some Cherokee remedy. But, here, it won't hurt anything. I've done it before."

Jonathan finally took the tiny splinter but he dropped it. "Well, I suppose that's the end of that. I dropped it," he said, looking about the stone floor.

Mandie looked at him and sighed. "Never mind. Let's work some more on this box," she said.

As the three turned back to the box, Mandie saw Snowball once again at work on the straw. The box she had tied him to was near enough that he could reach the cracked one.

"Move back and don't say a word. Snowball will do the work for us," Mandie said softly to her friends as she motioned them back.

The three watched as Snowball began getting large clumps of straw out from between the crack in the box. He meowed a little, growled a little, and fiercely clawed at the straw.

"I wonder what he's growling at," Celia whispered.

"He does that when he's angry," Mandie said softly. "But I don't know what he's angry about unless the straw has some odor on it he doesn't like."

The three sniffed the air and then laughed.

"I can't smell the straw from here," Mandie said.

Jonathan quickly reached behind Snowball and snatched a few strands of the straw he had removed from the box. He held it up to his nose and announced, "It smells like fish."

"Fish?" Mandie questioned. "I don't think there could be fish in those boxes. They'd be all rotten. The boxes might have been on a fishing boat and picked up the odor from that."

"But we can't smell the boxes in here. There is no fish odor in this room," Celia remarked.

"You're right, so whatever is inside the boxes must have the fish odor on it," Mandie decided.

"I can't imagine what could be in the boxes and have a fish odor," Jonathan said.

Suddenly there was a loud noise overhead as though someone were rattling heavy chains. The three young people froze as they listened. Then the sound stopped.

Mandie tried to see through a grill at the top of the wall, but it was too small and too far up.

She whispered to her friends as the noise continued, "This room must be under a building or a street, like a cellar. Maybe we could pile the boxes high enough to see out the grill."

"Good idea," Jonathan said, stepping over to the stack against the wall. "We can just add to these and make it high enough."

"But we'll have to make a few lower stacks so we can climb up on them," Mandie said.

The three quickly worked together, lifting and stacking the boxes until they were near the grill overhead.

"I'll climb up and look out," Jonathan said as he

stepped onto a lower stack of boxes.

"Be careful," Celia warned him.

The girls watched until Jonathan had reached the top. Then he tried to see through the grill. "I can't see anything. There's something blocking the outside."

"Then let's move the boxes over to another grill," Mandie told him.

They again moved and stacked the boxes until they reached another grill in the wall. Jonathan climbed up on top of them.

"All I can see is a stone wall outside or something like that," Jonathan called down to the girls. He twisted his head this way and that trying to look out.

"Let's try another grill," Mandie told him.

The three again moved the stack under another grill and Jonathan climbed up to the grill. "This is better," Jonathan told them. "I can see what must be an alleyway."

"An alleyway?" Mandie said. "Let me look." She began climbing upon the boxes, and just as Jonathan reached out his hand to help her, the stack swayed and the two found themselves falling in the middle of all the heavy boxes.

The boxes landed with a loud bang on the stone floor. Jonathan and Mandie, holding to each other, managed to stay on top. Celia had run to a corner of the room to avoid the falling boxes.

She hurried over to them. "Are y'all all right?" she asked.

Mandie stretched and stood up on a box. Jonathan jumped down and helped her off.

"I think I'm all right," Mandie said, shaking out her crumpled skirt and adjusting her displaced bonnet.

"I am, too," Jonathan said. "But look what a mess we

made. Now we'll have to at least stack the boxes to get them out of the way."

"But I didn't get to look outside," Mandie protested.

"There was nothing out there to see but a deserted old street," Jonathan told her as he bent to pick up a box.

"Well, I'd still like to see it," Mandie insisted as she helped with the boxes. "Let's stack all these back under that grill."

"If you insist," Jonathan said with a shrug.

Mandie added, "I haven't heard that clanking noise up there anymore."

"Whatever it was we probably scared it away with all that loud banging when the boxes tumbled down," Celia remarked as she grasped a heavy box with Mandie.

"And I wonder why some of these boxes didn't split open when they fell," Mandie remarked as she looked at each box they stacked.

"The metal bands hold them together and the wood is awfully thick," Jonathan told her as he hoisted a box to the top of the stack.

"Mandie, I am worried about getting back to the hotel," Celia remarked as they worked. "Your grandmother and the senator will be back and won't know where we are."

Mandie laughed a little nervously. "But we don't know where we are either. If we could get up to that grill and attract someone's attention, maybe we could get out."

The three worked faster and were getting covered with dirt from the boxes and the stone floor where they had been sitting. The girls had pushed their bonnets back to hang on the strings.

Mandie suddenly remembered her kitten and almost dropped the box she and Celia were carrying. "Where is Snowball? Help me find him!" she anxiously cried, looking around the room. She and Celia set the box down, and they all began searching.

In the jumble of boxes, Mandie finally found the one Snowball had been clawing at. He was not there.

"I don't remember seeing him when all the boxes came falling down," Celia told her.

"He's got to be here somewhere," Mandie insisted as she continued searching. "Snowball, where are you? Kitty, kitty, kitty!"

There was a faint meow. The three stood still, listening.

"Over there," Jonathan said, pointing toward the box Snowball had been working on.

Mandie bent to look around and could not find him. "Snowball! Come here! Kitty, kitty, kitty!"

The meow came again, louder this time.

"He's inside that box!" Mandie exclaimed as she stooped to examine the place where he had been clawing the straw. "The hole is bigger!" She tried to reach inside through the straw but something blocked her way. Snowball began howling.

"I think the three of us could break the box open now," Jonathan said as he looked at it.

They gathered around the cracked place, and with each one pulling at the cracked wood the box began splintering away. Suddenly Snowball jumped out through a wad of straw. Mandie picked him up.

"You naughty kitten," she scolded him. "You had me worried."

"Look!" Jonathan said, excitedly pulling straw from the crushed box.

The girls watched as he uncovered what looked like several large stones in the box. As the last of the straw came out, he pulled out what was indeed a rock, then another, another and another.

"Nothing but rocks in the box!" Mandie exclaimed as Snowball managed to break from her grasp. He ran to the rocks and began sniffing at them.

"And they do smell like fish," Celia said.

"Why would anyone want to pack up just plain old rocks?" Mandie asked.

Jonathan was thoroughly examining the box. "I have no idea, but that is all that was in the box," he said, standing up and brushing off his pants.

"Do you suppose all these boxes have rocks in them?" Celia asked as the three looked about the room.

"Probably so, but it would be too big a job to find out for sure," Jonathan said.

"This is plain crazy!" Mandie exclaimed. "Do these Belgium people sell boxes of rocks or something?"

"Maybe they are some historical rocks, worth money," Celia suggested.

Mandie reached down and picked up Snowball. "Here, Snowball, put your nose to use. Smell these boxes." She held him in her arms as she put his nose next to each box. The cat wriggled to get down and didn't show the least interest in the other ones.

"Evidently he can't smell anything in the other boxes," Jonathan said.

Mandie set him down and watched. He went straight to the crushed box and began smelling the stones that had come out of it.

"I'd say that box was the only one that smelled like fish," Mandie said. "Come on. Now that I know he's all right, I still want to climb up there and look through the grill."

As soon as they were able to stack the boxes high enough, Mandie lifted her long skirts and carefully climbed up, first on the low stack, then onto a higher stack, and finally to the highest one. The grill was a little far from her because of her short height, so she tried to stand on her tiptoes to see outside.

Suddenly the door to the room was flung open and banged back against the wall. The young people gasped as they saw the strange woman standing there. The woman had first appeared on the ship to Europe and turned up in various places they had visited since then. She was old, with gray hair showing around her black bonnet, and a diamond broach pinning her expensive black dress. Her black eyes looked directly at Mandie as she said, "You must get out of here at once. Immediately! Now!"

Mandie quickly asked, "Why?" She lost her balance at that moment. The stack of boxes swayed and she fell off. Luckily she landed on her feet. Jonathan and Celia rushed to her rescue.

"Are you all right?" they both asked.

Mandie quickly pushed them aside and looked for the woman in the doorway. She was gone. The door still stood open.

"Where did that woman go?" Mandie asked, running to look outside into the next room.

She dashed back, grabbed up Snowball, and yelled to her friends, "Come on! Let's find her!"

Mandie ran through the outer room and into the tunnel. She looked about, but there was no sign of the woman. "Oh, where did she go?"

"And how did she know we were in that room?" Jonathan asked.

"And how did she open the door when we couldn't?" Celia asked.

The three stood there puzzled.

"I suppose we could look for her, but we never do find her when she appears like that. It's like she's a ghost or something, the way she manages to evade us," Mandie complained, holding on to Snowball.

"Well, let's get out of this tunnel," Jonathan said, leading the way back in the direction of the hotel.

As the three emerged into the bright sunlight, they realized everyone seemed to be staring at them. Then Mandie glanced down at their clothes. They were all filthy dirty. Her hands looked as though they'd never been washed. Even Snowball's white fur was soiled.

"Oh, look at us! How are we ever going to get back into the hotel to our rooms without everyone seeing us?" Mandie exclaimed, stopping at the corner of the alleyway.

"Every building must have a back door," Jonathan said. "And we can probably find one to the hotel."

"I sure hope so," Mandie said.

Celia quickly looked at the watch she wore on a chain around her neck and breathed a sigh of relief. "At least it's nowhere time for your grandmother and the senator to come back. In fact, we have plenty of time to clean up before we eat."

"Thank goodness!" Mandie said as they hurried on.

Jonathan led the way. They darted behind trees and shrubbery bushes to avoid being seen by hotel guests who were strolling outside. Finally he discovered a back door and pushed it open.

The door led directly into the huge corridor, and the young people ran for the stairs. They managed to arrive at their rooms without attracting attention.

"Jonathan, give us a few minutes to clean up and change clothes and we'll meet you at the landing," Mandie told him as she and Celia opened the door to their suite.

"I have to do the same," Jonathan agreed as he went on down the corridor.

Mandie removed the leash and set Snowball down on the carpet. He immediately went to work washing his white fur.

The girls quickly bathed and put on clean clothes. They talked as they hurried.

"Things sure are getting complicated," Mandie remarked as she slipped into a dark blue dress. "There are so many mysteries. Do you suppose they could all be connected in some way?"

"I don't know," Celia replied as she buttoned her brown dress. "I sure wish we'd had on these dark dresses this morning when we got so dirty."

"When you think about it, there's the robbery of that painting, then the man we saw with a painting here in the hotel, and the man on the old boat, and the boxes in that room we were in, and then the strange woman appearing," Mandie said, brushing her long blond hair. "And I don't know what else. If we could just figure out one little clue to it all, we might be able to solve everything."

"I don't imagine your grandmother will want to stay here much longer, because this is our third day in Antwerp and we still have other countries to visit and not a whole lot of time left," Celia said as she, too, began brushing her long auburn hair.

"And Uncle Ned hasn't even gotten here yet," Mandie said, suddenly remembering. "He did say he would be here sooner or later. I wish he'd come soon."

"When we meet Jonathan at the landing, what are we going to do next?" Celia asked.

"Well, I just don't know," Mandie replied. "We'll have to talk it over and see which angle of this mystery would be the best to follow up."

"Whatever we do, Mandie, please, let's be here when your grandmother gets back," Celia said, turning to look at her friend.

"I've planned to do that all morning. However, sometimes circumstances prevent our carrying out our plans, like that locked room," Mandie said, walking about the room. "That is really a puzzle to me. I just can't imagine why anyone would pack rocks in straw and box them up in nice big, strong wooden boxes with metal bands around them."

Celia looked thoughtful for a moment and then said, "You know, Mandie, I have heard of whole buildings being shipped stone by stone."

"But I don't think the other boxes had stones in them. At least Snowball wasn't interested in sniffing them," Mandie said, looking down at the kitten, who was pretty white again. He was now washing his paws.

"I'm ready," Celia said, picking up the bonnet that matched her dress.

"Then let's go talk this over with Jonathan and decide what to do next," Mandie said. She took her dark blue bonnet from her hatbox and hastily put it on. "And I suppose I'll have to take Snowball. Someone might let him out. And he did help us by pulling the straw out of that box." She picked him up and fastened on his leash.

The girls hurried to meet Jonathan at the landing to make plans.

Chapter 9 / The Same Mistake Twice

Jonathan was waiting for them on the stairway. The girls dropped down on the steps near him. Mandie wrapped Snowball's leash around her wrist to keep him from getting away.

"Things are really popping!" Jonathan exclaimed. "I just heard the maids talking down the hallway there. Another painting was stolen from another museum. And the first painting hasn't even been recovered yet."

"Goodness gracious!" Mandie said. "This just can't go on. Whoever is doing this will soon have a stolen fortune if we don't find them."

"I think we'd better let the police find them, Mandie. They could be dangerous," Celia commented.

"But we probably know more than the police," Mandie disagreed, as Snowball rubbed around her ankles. "I'm almost positive that's the thief we've been seeing. We just have to catch up with him."

"Well, so far that's been impossible," Jonathan said.

"And we also have to find out what's in those boxes in that tunnel room and why that strange woman from the ship suddenly appeared and warned us to leave," Mandie said.

"And who locked the door after we went into the room," Celia added.

"I just can't imagine why anyone would pack up rocks in a wooden box like we found," Jonathan said.

"And the man, Alex, on the old boat. He's a mystery that we need to solve. I kinda believe all these things must be connected. I don't know how, but I think if we can solve one part, just any part, then we'll be able to figure out the rest," Mandie said.

"You know, you may be right. Just think of it this way," Jonathan agreed. "We followed the man into the tunnel, or alleyway, and then we found the room with the boxes right along the pathway he probably took. And if this is the same man who visits Alex on the old boat, then the two of them must be crooks of some kind, stealing paintings, or whatever."

"I wonder what the thief will do with the paintings," Celia remarked.

"He'd probably have to ship them out of the country in order to sell them. So you see that would work out right with Alex on that old boat. He could haul them out," Mandie said.

"Mandie, I doubt that boat could be used. It looks as though it's not safe," Jonathan said.

"Well, then Alex could have another boat somewhere, or some connection with another boat," Mandie said.

"Maybe," Jonathan said. "But what do you think causes Alex to cry so much? It isn't normal for a big man like that to lie on a bunk all day, sobbing his heart out."

"I know. That's one thing I can't figure out. Maybe he's

sick or something," Mandie said.

"He keeps telling the man who visits him that he's guilty," Celia reminded her friends.

"Yes, and guilty of what?" Mandie said. "But the man who comes to the boat keeps telling him he's not guilty. If he had anything to do with the theft of the paintings, he'd certainly be guilty, but I can't imagine why he'd cry about it."

"Maybe he's sorry he did such a dishonest thing and now there would be no way for him to be forgiven without getting into trouble with the law," Celia suggested.

"Oh, this is such a puzzle," said Mandie, sighing loudly. "I'd just like to catch that strange woman from the ship and hold her still long enough to make her tell us what she's up to, following us around all the time."

"Me, too," Jonathan agreed.

"I don't know how she can figure out where we are going to be, the way she turns up everywhere," Celia said. "We don't even know from one minute to the next where we're headed."

"We still have time before we eat. Let's go back toward the old boat and keep our eyes open for that man we've been seeing," Mandie said as she stood up and straightened her long skirts.

"And for that strange woman, now that we know she's here in Antwerp," Jonathan added as he and Celia got up.

The three hurried down the stairs to the reception room. They looked everywhere to be sure the strange woman or the man was not around. Then they searched the tea parlor, the drawing room, and finally left by the front door.

Outside they stood on the sidewalk and watched passersby. No one looked familiar. Slowly strolling down the avenue, they headed in the direction of the wharf.

"We also need to keep a lookout for Uncle Ned. He may get here and we won't know it," Mandie told her friends. "And we sure could use him right now to help us solve all these mysteries."

"Won't he be staying at the hotel with us?" Jonathan asked.

"He knows where we are and he said he'd catch up with us but he didn't know when," Mandie replied. Snowball walked along at the end of his leash beside her.

"I think we'd better check with the clerk at the hotel once in a while to be sure he hasn't arrived and gone on up to his room without our knowing it," Celia said.

"We can later, but knowing Uncle Ned, he'll find us," Mandie said.

The young people didn't see anyone familiar and finally made their way to the old boat. They silently climbed on board and crept behind the trash pile to watch and listen. Mandie held Snowball tightly in her arms.

"Let's see if the man is inside," Mandie whispered to her friends. She cautiously led the way to the broken window. They peeped inside. The man seemed to be asleep on the bunk bed. After watching quietly for a few minutes, the three returned to their hiding place on the deck.

"No telling how long he'll sleep. Let's go back to the room in the tunnel," Mandie said softly.

Jonathan and Celia followed her down the ladder and up to the pier. They walked down the long plank floor to the street. Then they stopped to talk.

"I don't see any reason to go back to that room in the tunnel," Jonathan said as they stood there.

"I'd like to find out what's in all those boxes," Mandie said as she put Snowball down, still on his leash.

Jonathan blew out his breath and said, "There's no way we can get those boxes open, Mandie. You know we tried."

"We can get some tools from somewhere to work on them," Mandie said.

"Tools?" he questioned.

"Like a hammer. We could bust them open with a hammer," Mandie replied.

"You can't do that!" Jonathan objected. "You might bust open whatever is inside them."

"Well, we could try to pull the metal bands off. That would make it easier to get the boxes open," Mandie said.

"Don't forget about that door," Celia reminded them. "We got locked in there, remember? And someone might lock us inside again."

"We can prop the door open with some of the boxes," Mandie told her.

"But then anyone who passes by the doorway could see what we're doing and we could get in trouble, because those boxes belong to someone," Jonathan told her.

"Oh, Jonathan, if you're ever going to be a detective, you've got to learn that you have to take chance," Mandie said, exasperated with his objections. "Now let's look around until we find a hammer."

Mandie led the way along the row of shops. She couldn't see any business that might sell hammers. And she didn't want to ask for one until she found the right place. No use in spreading the word that they were looking for a hammer. Best to keep their doings secret.

"There must not be any tool shops anywhere near," she remarked as they came to the end of the street. "At home you can always find a store with all kinds of tools in it." The three stopped to talk.

"This is a city, Mandie. They don't need tools like the

farmers do back where you come from," Jonathan said.

"I live in Franklin, North Carolina, and that is a city, Jonathan Guyer," Mandie said, impatiently stomping her foot. "The farmers come to town to buy their tools and supplies."

"But this is not the United States, and these people here have their own way of doing things," Jonathan told her. "The only place I can think of where we could possibly borrow a hammer is back at the hotel."

"At the hotel?" Mandie questioned. Then she nodded her head. "You're right. They have to have tools to keep everything in working order."

"And how are we going to borrow a hammer, Mandie, from the hotel? They'll just say they will fix whatever needs a hammer," Celia said.

Mandie thought for a moment and then said with a smile, "We'll just say we want to borrow a hammer to crack nuts. That'll do. Come on."

The three hurried back to the hotel and up to the clerk at the desk. He looked at them questioningly and didn't speak. Mandie cleared her throat and asked, "Mister, could we borrow a hammer?"

The man raised his eyebrows and said, "Something needs hammer to fix?"

"No, no, no," Mandie quickly replied. "We have some nuts that we need a hammer to crack."

"Nuts, hammer crack?" the man said. He bent to reach inside a cabinet under the desk and came up with a small hammer that he held out to Mandie. "Must be big nuts that need hammer to crack."

"Yes, sir, thank you." Mandie took the hammer and hurried toward the stairs. Jonathan and Celia followed.

Mandie paused at the bottom of the steps and said, "I'll go get a scarf to wrap this hammer in so the man

won't see us taking it out of the hotel. I'll be right back."
She handed Snowball's leash to Celia and carried the
hammer with her.

She ran up the stairs two at a time, rushed into her
room, snatched up a red silk scarf, and hurried back
downstairs. By the time she reached her friends, she had
the hammer securely covered with the scarf.

Jonathan looked at the scarf and said, "Why didn't
you get a dark colored scarf? That red attracts attention."

"Because this is the only one I could find in a hurry,"
Mandie replied. "Would you hold on to Snowball for me,
Celia, and I'll carry the hammer, like this." She held the
tool up in her arms to keep the scarf from revealing its
contents. "Let's go."

The three hurried down the avenue and on to the
alleyway where the tunnel began. They found the door,
opened it, and crossed the room to open the door to the
smaller room where they had found the boxes. They
paused.

"We'd better be real quiet about this just in case
someone is inside," Mandie whispered to her friends as
she stood there with her hand on the door latch.

"Right," Jonathan agreed while Celia nodded her
head and held on to Snowball's leash.

Mandie pushed on the door and nothing happened.
She pushed harder without any luck. Jonathan and Celia
reached to help. Even with the pressure from all three of
the young people the door wouldn't budge.

"It must be locked," Mandie whispered with a sigh.
"Can y'all hear anything inside?"

The three stood there listening, but no sound came
from the room.

"Let's get bold," Mandie said, lifting the hammer. "I'll
pound with the hammer while y'all push real hard on the
door. Ready?"

"Someone will hear us," Celia protested.

"And we'll get into trouble," Jonathan said.

"Oh, come on and help me," Mandie said. "We can't hear anything inside. Therefore, there must not be anyone in there. This whole tunnel place seems to be deserted. There's nobody around to see or hear us."

Jonathan shrugged his shoulders. "Well, all right."

Celia said, "I suppose if y'all insist on doing this, I'll have to help." She looked around the room. "I'll tie Snowball over here to the door we came in so I can use both hands. Wait a minute." She hurried back to the other door, looped Snowball's leash around the handle, and came back to help Mandie and Jonathan.

"Ready?" Mandie asked as she raised the hammer.

Her friends nodded as they pushed with all their might on the door and Mandie began pounding on it. She kept missing the door and hitting the door facing with the hammer, but suddenly the door swung open.

"I knew we could do it!" Mandie cried, excitedly entering the room, which was still full of boxes. "Come on."

"Not until I make sure this door can't close and lock us in again," Jonathan said as he looked around.

Celia had gone back to get Snowball and now she offered to hold the door open. "I could just stand here leaning against it while y'all hammer on those boxes. That way it won't close," she said as she stepped back to hold it open.

"All right," Mandie agreed as she walked among the stacks of boxes. Turning to Jonathan she asked, "Which one should we start on?"

"I guess any one would do," Jonathan said. "You're probably going to break whatever is in it anyway."

Mandie raised the hammer as she stopped before a box. "Here goes!" she said as she brought the tool down on the wooden box, and watched for the wood to crack.

But the box didn't even move, much less crack. Mandie tried again, still with no results at all.

"Let me try," Jonathan offered. "I'm a little stronger than you are."

Mandie gave him the hammer and she watched as he swung it down again and again on the box without making a splinter.

"I don't think this hammer is strong enough," Jonathan said after a futile try at breaking open the box. The metal bands held tight. He laid down the hammer.

"There's got to be some way to get these boxes open," Mandie complained as she looked around the room. Crossing over to the box they had broken open earlier, she stooped and looked at the rocks that had been in it. "Why don't we use these big rocks to try to smash one open?" She couldn't lift the large one.

"Wait, I'll help you," Jonathan told her. He grasped one end of the rock while she took the other. Together they walked back to the box they had been pounding with the hammer.

"When I say one, two, three, let's drop it together on the box," Mandie said.

"Go ahead," Jonathan told her.

"One, two, three," Mandie repeated and she and Jonathan swung the heavy rock down on the box. They bent quickly to examine it. The wood was slightly splintered in one place. "I think it will break it open if we keep on doing this," she said.

"There's no telling what's in this box, Mandie, so get prepared to jump away from it. The contents could come flying everywhere if we break it open," Jonathan warned her as he helped her lift the huge rock again.

"One, two, three," Mandie again said, and they threw

the rock down on the box again.

"Y'all are making an awful noise," Celia told them as she held on to Snowball, who was excited by the racket.

"I know, but we'll soon have this open," Mandie said as she and Jonathan once again lifted the rock and smashed the box.

This time there was a loud cracking sound, and the two jumped back as the box splintered into pieces. Then Mandie rushed forward to see what was inside. She quickly pulled at the straw stuffing. Her fingers met something hard and cold.

"There's something in here!" she cried excitedly, digging at the straw.

"Of course there's something in there," Jonathan told her as he helped.

Celia moved forward to see, but she kept her foot against the door to prevent it from closing.

Mandie suddenly sat back on to the floor and exclaimed, "Rocks again! Nothing but rocks! Just like the other box."

"All that hard work for nothing," Jonathan grumbled as he sat beside her.

"Well, now that y'all know there're rocks in the boxes, why don't we go back to the hotel? It must be time to eat," Celia said.

Mandie quickly stood up. "No, let's try just one more box. One that's in a different stack," she said, walking around to look at the jumbled boxes.

Jonathan sighed. "All right, one more but no more than that. I agree with Celia. I'm getting awfully hungry."

"This one," Mandie said, pulling on a box at the top of a stack. "Let's get this one down on the floor and try it."

She and Jonathan pulled at the box but the whole stack wobbled.

"They're all going to fall down, Mandie," Jonathan warned.

"And that would make a terrible racket," Celia added.

"All right then. Let's try this one," Mandie said, bending to look at another box that was sitting by itself on the floor. "They all look alike, the same size and shape."

"And they probably all have rocks in them," Jonathan added as he, too, stooped to inspect the box.

"Why don't y'all pull a box over here to prop open the door and I'll help you. We can tie Snowball back there out of the way behind the stacks," Celia offered.

"Good idea," Mandie said. "Jonathan, let's push this box over there."

Jonathan helped and they soon had slid the box in front of the open door. Celia went around behind the stacks and tied Snowball's leash to one of the metal bands on a box.

"Now let's get that big rock and try it on this box," Mandie said, leading the way over to the rock they had used.

It was easier to lift with the three working together, and they began pounding the box with the rock. Nothing seemed to happen.

Mandie straightened up for a moment. "Should we try another box? This one seems awfully hard to crack. And not only that—" She stopped suddenly and whispered quickly to her friends. "I hear someone coming! Let's hide!"

The three quickly darted around behind the boxes where Snowball was tied and where they would be out of sight to anyone passing the doorway. Mandie's heartbeat quickened as she heard loud, heavy footsteps coming nearer. They paused at the open doorway. She could just barely peek through an opening between the stacks of boxes. Her heart did a flip-flop when she saw two men in police uniform standing there.

Mandie held on to Snowball to keep him from making a noise as she listened to the two men talking loudly in what she recognized as French even though she couldn't understand a word of it. Jonathan and Celia huddled close-by and watched through the crack between the boxes.

Mandie saw the men quickly push the box away from the door and leave the room, slamming the door behind them. There was a click of the lock. She gasped in fright. Now they would have to find a way out of this place again.

The three stood up, looked around the room, and groaned together. They were trapped!

"What did those policemen say?" Mandie quickly asked Jonathan.

"I couldn't understand everything, but they said they didn't know why this room was open and the door left ajar. Evidently they knew a man's name connected with this room but I missed that."

"So the police know about this room," Mandie said as she looked around and picked up the hammer.

"And I imagine they'll be going to find out from the man they mentioned why it was open," Jonathan added.

"And we're stuck in here," Celia said. She had quickly moved across the room to try the door. It wouldn't open.

Mandie rushed up behind her and also tried it.

"Don't worry. We'll get out somehow," she said, not exactly believing it herself this time.

The strange woman from the ship had rescued them before. Maybe the woman would come to their aid again. Or just maybe they could force the door open somehow.

Chapter 10 / Caught!

The three young people beat and banged on the door, but it would not open. Mandie used the hammer on it without any luck. They made so much noise it was a wonder no one heard them.

"Let's beat on the boxes while we figure out how to get out of here," Mandie suggested as the three looked at one another in desperation.

She went back to the box they had been working on. Then she decided to move on to the next box. She raised the hammer and pounded on the metal bands around it. Jonathan and Celia watched.

Suddenly the box caved it. "Look!" Mandie cried excitedly, stooping to investigate the contents. "Look what's inside!" She frantically pulled at the straw stuffing, and her friends joined her. Finally they were able to pull out a smaller box. This box was not so hard to get into.

"Oh, it's a painting!" Mandie exclaimed as she held up a small framed object.

Jonathan examined it and said, "It's small but it is an original painting, I think."

"Yes, I believe it is, too," Celia agreed.

Mandie quickly scooped out the rest of the straw, but there was nothing else inside. She stood up and surveyed the stacks of boxes.

"Do y'all think we could open the rest of the boxes? They might contain more paintings," Mandie said as she walked around the boxes.

"But you know we found rocks before," Jonathan reminded her.

"I know but I'd guess that the rocks are only a decoy so all the boxes wouldn't weigh the same. And the rocks are so heavy no one would suspect that there were paintings in any of the boxes," Mandie explained. "I think we've found a smuggler's loot."

"Maybe, but where is the smuggler? He, or she, would probably be more important to the police than stolen paintings, because unless they catch him, or her, paintings might still be stolen," Jonathan said.

"If we can find out what's in these other boxes, though, and if there are paintings in them, we could always go tell the police, and they might catch the thief when he, or she, as you say, comes here to this room," Mandie argued. Turning to look at her two friends, she asked, "Well, are y'all with me or not?"

"Since we don't have anything else to do, we might as well crack open the boxes," Jonathan said with a sigh.

"I'll help since I can't hold the door this time," Celia offered.

The three began pounding on a nearby box with the large rock and with the hammer. The box burst open finally, exposing more rocks.

"Don't give up," Mandie told them. "I'm sure all the

boxes don't contain rocks." She climbed up on a stack nearby to pull off a box in the next row. As she did, the whole stack fell over and bounced against the door.

As the three watched the boxes fall, to their amazement the door sprang open. They quickly turned to hide from whoever opened the door. As they peeked from behind the stacks of boxes left standing, they watched for someone to enter. There was not a sound once the boxes settled down on the floor.

"Someone opened that door. Where are they?" Mandie whispered to her friends.

"I don't know, but I'd say now is the best chance we'll have to get out of this room," Jonathan said, standing up and quietly moving around the boxes toward the door.

"But what about the painting? Should we take it with us?" Mandie whispered loudly as she reached to pick it up.

"Not unless you want to be accused of stealing it," Jonathan said.

Mandie quickly dropped the painting onto the top of a nearby box. "You're right," she said. "Come on! Let's get out of here!" She picked up the hammer and pulled the red silk scarf from her pocket to wrap it.

"I'll take Snowball," Celia said, quickly picking up the kitten.

The three hesitated at the doorway. Mandie cautiously looked out into the other room and then went on to the doorway to the passageway. There was no one in sight.

"That door didn't open itself," Mandie said, coming back to look at the door. She examined the lock and then the connecting piece of the lock in the door facing. She was puzzled as she stood there mulling things over.

"Come on!" Jonathan urged her.

"Before someone comes," Celia added.

"Wait! I think I know what opened the door," Mandie told her friends as she still stood there surveying the door and the room. "Those boxes hit the door and it opened just like that. There has got to be some contraption to make the door open." She uncovered the hammer and began beating on the door facing. Finally she stopped and pointed. "Look! Here is a spring imbedded in the wooden door facing! Evidently when it's hit, it makes the door open. Let's try it and see if it works."

"No, no, no," Jonathan told her. "I'm not taking a chance of getting locked in that room again."

"And neither am I," Celia added as she quickly stepped outside into the passageway. She carried Snowball with her.

"All right then, I'll go back inside and shut the door and try it," Mandie told her friends as Jonathan joined Celia.

Mandie quickly shut the door while she stayed inside the room. Testing it to be sure it was locked, she pounded on the door facing where she had found the latch. The door immediately sprang open.

"You see?" she excitedly told her friends as they watched in surprise. "Now there must be another one on the outside." She examined the door facing on the passageway side. "Here it is. Let's shut it again and open it from this side."

As Jonathan and Celia watched, Mandie closed the door, then pounded on it with the hammer, and it immediately opened.

"How about that?" she said, smiling at her friends. "I've never seen anything like this before."

"Neither have I but, Mandie, come on. Let's go eat," Jonathan told her.

"Yes, someone might come down the corridor and

see us," Celia reminded her friend.

Jonathan and Celia started walking up the passageway. Mandie decided she had better join them.

As the three hurried toward the hotel, Mandie thought about the secret of the lock. She suddenly remembered Jonathan accidentally banging his head against the door when they had tried to open it before and then the door opened. Also this time she had pounded on the door with the hammer when they wanted to get into the room and the door had opened. Evidently the secret spring had been hit each time. Then she remembered the strange woman from the ship had opened the door.

"Wait a minute!" she said to her friends as she slowed down. "I've figured something out."

Jonathan and Celia stopped and turned to look at her. They listened as she explained about the lock. Then she added, "I wonder how that strange woman from the ship knew how to open the door. Remember she did open it?"

Jonathan and Celia were impressed with her deductions.

"Yes, she did," Celia agreed.

"But as far as that woman is concerned, how did she know we were in that room? In fact, how did she know we were even in Antwerp?" Jonathan asked.

"Sooner or later we're going to find out about that woman," Mandie decided as they continued to walk toward the hotel.

"Right now let's find out what the hotel has to eat," Jonathan said with his mischievous grin.

They went straight to the dining room and found it almost empty. Celia quickly looked at her watch and told them it was late to be eating the noon meal.

"I suppose they'll still have something to eat," Mandie

said as she laid the scarf-wrapped hammer on an extra chair next to her and took Snowball from her friend. She tied him to a table leg after the waiter had seated them.

"We certainly do have something to eat," the waiter said, smiling at her. He placed menus before them and told them what was still available.

They all ordered beef roast. It was the nearest thing to American they could find. Mandie hoped it would at least do them until suppertime.

"If we're late eating, I wonder if Grandmother and Senator Morton have gotten back yet," Mandie asked as the waiter wrote down their order.

"I could go ask the desk clerk," Jonathan offered.

"Never mind, I'll go. Be right back," Mandie said, getting up and leaving the room.

At the desk the attendant gave her a message from her grandmother. A messenger had brought a note for Mandie, saying Mrs. Taft and Senator Morton had been delayed and that it would be late afternoon before they returned. Mandie read it and rushed back to the table.

"Grandmother and the senator won't be back until late today," she said, waving the piece of paper at her friends. "That gives us time to go back to the boat again before they come back."

"Do you think we ought to take a chance going down there again? We might not get back before your grandmother does," Celia said.

"We won't stay long," Mandie promised. "I'd just like to see if that other man comes back to visit the one on the boat, because I think that other man is definitely the thief who stole the painting."

The waiter had come back with glasses of water they had ordered. He looked at Mandie and asked, "Do you speak of a thief who stole the paintings out of two museums?"

Mandie looked up at him and said, "Yes, the man who stole the Rubens painting and another one from another museum. I think I've seen him."

"That thief was just caught today. His picture is in the newspaper," the waiter said.

"In the newspaper? Could we see it?" Mandie asked excitedly.

"Of course," the waiter said and rushed off to get it.

"I sure hope they got him. I want to see if he's the same man we've been seeing," Mandie said to her friends.

"They certainly did catch the thief fast," Jonathan remarked. "But then I've heard they have an excellent police force in this city."

The waiter returned with the newspaper and spread it out on the table before Mandie. She quickly looked at the photograph on the front page and said, "That's the man. That's the one we've been seeing."

Jonathan and Celia bent over to see.

"That does look like the man we've seen," Celia remarked.

"It's probably the same man," Jonathan agreed.

Mandie picked up the newspaper and offered it back to the waiter. The man shook his head. "You may keep the paper, if you like. We've all read it. Now I'll get your food." He left the room as Mandie thanked him for the paper.

"Now we don't have to go back down to the old boat," Celia said.

"Oh yes, we must," Mandie told her. "You see, we've got to find out if the police also took the man called Alex."

"Then we'd better hurry," Celia said.

The waiter brought the food and the three young people ate so fast they didn't really pay much attention to what they were eating. But they also cleaned every crumb from their plates. Mandie fed Snowball under the table. Finally they were ready to go. Mandie picked up Snowball and the hammer and carried them both. Celia took the newspaper.

As they hurried outside, Mandie turned to her friends and said, "Let's go by way of the tunnel, just to see if the door to that room is still standing open like we left it."

"Oh, Mandie," Jonathan protested. "I know you. When we get to the room, you're going to want to break open more boxes and we'll never get back to the hotel."

"No, I promise," Mandie protested. "I only want to look and then we'll go on to the old boat."

"I'll make sure you keep your promise," Jonathan said with his mischievous grin as they walked along the avenue.

They had the route memorized by now, so they were soon at the room in the tunnel. As they approached, Mandie ran ahead and exclaimed, "The door is still open!" She had crossed the room off the passageway and was looking into the smaller room where the boxes still lay scattered about.

Jonathan caught up with her and said, "Now you've seen that the door is still open so let's go on."

"Let me just look and see if that little painting is still there where we took it out of the box," Mandie insisted as she hurried inside the room and around the stacks of boxes.

The painting still lay on top of a box where they had left it. Evidently no one had entered the room since they had been gone.

"All right, it's not been disturbed. Let's go on," Mandie told her friends as she came out into the passageway and led the way toward the old boat.

When they arrived at the wharf, they hurried down the

pier and used the rope ladders to board the old boat. They slipped over the side and crept behind the trash pile on the deck where they could watch and listen. There was no sound from the cabin.

"I'm going to see if Alex is still here," Mandie whispered to her friends. She handed Snowball to Celia and the hammer to Jonathan. Then she slowly moved toward the window of the cabin. Just as she reached it she heard someone coming up the rope ladder. Rushing back to her friends, she made a sign to them to be quiet.

As she heard the footsteps on the deck, Mandie quietly moved enough to see who it was. To her amazement it was the man they had seen before. He was carrying a package, as he always seemed to do. She snatched the newspaper from Celia and quickly compared the photograph with the man. It had to be the same person. If the police had arrested the man, he must have managed to break out of jail.

Jonathan and Celia also looked at the newspaper and at the man and nodded to Mandie.

The man went inside the cabin and the young people immediately heard Alex yelling at him, "I told you not to come back anymore! I don't want you on my boat. Now begone!"

"Alex, Alex, you need help and I can give it to you," the man insisted.

"Begone!" Alex yelled. "I prefer living alone with my guilt!"

"But, Alex, you are not guilty," the other man insisted. "Why won't you listen to me? I want to help you."

"I do not want your help. I want to be alone," Alex insisted loudly. "Now, begone with you!"

Mandie heard them come out on the deck, and she strained to watch. Alex was shaking his fist. The other man was slowly backing away from him.

"I will come again later. Maybe you will eventually listen to me," the other man said as he started down the rope ladder.

"Do not come back!" Alex shouted as he returned to the cabin.

Mandie crept toward the edge of the boat. "It's safe. Let's follow him!" she whispered to her friends.

Jonathan and Celia followed her off the boat and down the pier. There she stopped to look around. The man had evaded them again.

"He's just evaporated again!" Mandie exclaimed as she stood there looking around.

"He's too fast for us. He knows his way around," Jonathan told her.

"Well, I suppose we'd better go back to the hotel," Mandie decided. "Let's cut through the tunnel on our way back."

"What for?" Jonathan asked.

"It's shorter and I like the tunnel. It's interesting," she said. "When we get time I'd like to explore the rest of it."

"I'd say we don't have time to explore right now," Celia spoke up.

They hurried back into the tunnel, and when they came to the room they had passed through before, all three of them stopped in surprise. The man they had just seen on the old boat was inside the room with the boxes.

"Sh-h-h-h!" Mandie cautioned her friends as she motioned them back from the doorway.

They huddled just outside the door and watched to see what the man was doing. He seemed to be looking all around the room and examining the boxes. Then he picked up the small painting they had found and left there.

"Aha!" he muttered to himself as he examined the painting.

Mandie held her breath and waited to see what he would do with it. He suddenly put it back where he had found it and turned to leave the room. The three young people nearly stumbled over one another as they rushed down the passageway toward the hotel. Mandie kept turning her head to see if the man was coming their way, but evidently he had gone the other direction. He was not in sight.

As they left the tunnel they stopped to talk.

"We've got to find the police and tell them we saw this man. He must have escaped from jail," Mandie told her friends. "And we need to tell them what we found in that room."

"But they already know about that room. They locked us in, remember?" Jonathan reminded her.

"They probably don't know about the rocks and the painting we found in the boxes," Mandie insisted.

"If we tell them about all that, they'll know we were the ones who smashed the boxes," Celia warned her.

"But wouldn't they appreciate the fact that we found the thief for them and also found where the paintings are evidently being smuggled out?" Mandie asked.

"You never know. This is not the United States and they may not think like we do back home," Jonathan said. "Besides, those two policemen we saw seemed to know about that room, and they might just know what is going on."

"Oh, everything has become twisted up!" Mandie exclaimed as she let Snowball down to walk, his leash securely attached. She was still carrying the hammer. "Anyway, we've got to find some nuts. Let's discuss this while we look for some nuts."

"Nuts?" Jonathan and Celia both asked as they looked at her in surprise.

"Nuts," Mandie repeated. "Remember I told the man in the hotel that I wanted the hammer to crack some nuts. Well, I have to find some nuts and crack them with the hammer so I won't be telling a lie because he'll probably ask me if I was able to use the hammer."

"Mandie, the way you get around things!" Celia exclaimed.

"Honestly, when I borrowed the hammer I immediately thought of cracking nuts with it, so I think I'd like some nuts, anyway. Let's start looking for some place that sells nuts," she told her friends.

They walked slowly along the avenue, looking into various shops for nuts. There didn't seem to be anyone who sold them. Then finally Mandie spotted a sidewalk vendor ahead.

"I'd think he'd have some kind of nuts," she told her friends as she hurried to see.

The man did sell nuts. She bought a bagful of walnuts. Jonathan watched and he remarked, "You'll sure need the hammer to crack those walnuts."

"I know. I've had walnuts before. They grew in our yard back home at Charley Gap where I lived with my father," Mandie told him. "Let's go sit on the bench over there in the little park and crack nuts while we talk."

She led the way across the road to an empty bench beside a huge masonry water fountain. She tied Snowball's leash to the leg of the bench as her friends sat down beside her.

"I see a good place to crack the nuts—right here," she said, moving to sit on the foundation of the huge fountain. She spread out the red silk scarf on the grass to hold the cracked nuts.

"Are you going to eat those nuts?" Celia asked as she sat beside her.

"Sure. Nuts are brain food. They'll help me think better," Mandie said with a little laugh.

"I suppose that's some old Indian saying," Jonathan said, joining the girls on the foundation.

Mandie thought for a moment. She couldn't really remember where she'd heard such a thing, but she had heard other people claim nuts were brain food.

"I suppose so," she finally answered. "Now let's put our thinking caps on. We've got important decisions to make and we're going to have to hurry." She began cracking the hard-shelled walnuts.

Chapter 11 / Alex Talks

After much discussion the three young people decided to return to the hotel just long enough to give back the hammer Mandie had borrowed and check for any more messages that might have come.

Mandie, carrying the red silk scarf full of cracked walnuts, approached the man at the desk. "We used your hammer to crack all these nuts. Would you care for any?" she asked him. She opened the scarf to show him.

"All of those nuts were cracked with the hammer?" the man asked.

"Yes, sir, and here's your hammer," Jonathan told him as he handed over the hammer, which he had been carrying. "Thank you, sir."

"I am glad to know hammers can be used for cracking nuts," the man said with a smile. "But I do not wish any of the nuts, thank you."

Mandie hastily rolled up the scarf with the walnuts inside and asked, "Do we have any more messages?

Maybe from my grandmother?"

The man looked in the pigeonhole behind him and replied, "No, no messages for you."

"Thank you," Mandie replied as she turned to her two friends. "Ready?"

"Yes," Celia said as Jonathan nodded and started toward the front door.

Once outside the hotel they began looking for a policeman. Mandie had finally talked them into going to the police about the room in the tunnel and the man who visited the bearded man on the old boat.

"Any other time we'd see a policeman," Mandie complained as they walked and walked, up one side and down the other on the avenue.

"Maybe it's just not meant that we should tell the police," Celia suggested.

"I don't believe they have any policemen in this district," Jonathan said. "Mandie, couldn't we do something else, something more productive?"

"Like just walking into the cabin of that old boat and talking to the man named Alex?" Mandie asked as she stopped to look at him. Snowball trailed along on his leash. Jonathan and Celia also stopped.

"Well, all right, we could do that," Jonathan agreed.

"But Alex chases everyone off," Celia reminded them. "And if he's a criminal he could be dangerous."

"I don't think he looks dangerous. After all, he's just a big softhearted man the way he cries all the time," Mandie said.

"Well, if we're going, we'd better hurry instead of wasting time standing here talking about it," Jonathan reminded the girls as he started to walk on.

Mandie and Celia caught up with him, and this time they didn't go through the tunnel but stayed on the public streets to the wharf and then on to the pier. They hurriedly climbed the rope ladders and stepped onto the deck of the old boat. The loud sobbing sound they had heard before was coming from the cabin.

"Well, are we going inside?" Jonathan quietly asked Mandie as they stood there listening.

"Let's wait a few minutes and see if he hushes. I imagine he definitely would run us off if we surprised him while he's crying," Mandie said. She led the way to their hiding place behind the trash pile.

As the three stooped down to get out of sight, Snowball managed to get loose and run toward the cabin door. The three watched as he slipped through the partly open door. Then they hurried to the window to look inside.

Mandie could see the man lying on the bunk bed as he cried and stared at the ceiling. Snowball came into view as he smelled around the room and finally jumped upon the man's bed. Hesitating for a moment, the kitten twitched his ears and then crept up to the man's face and snuggled down beside him. Mandie's heart raced. The man might hurt Snowball!

"I have to go get him," she told her friends.

But as Mandie turned to walk around to the door, she saw the man rub Snowball's fur and then sit up to hold him in his arms.

"And here I thought I dreamed about you, but here you are," Alex said to the cat as he held him up against his face. "You can't be my baby's kitten. He had one black speck on his face, right there." He looked into Snowball's eyes and rubbed his face. "My baby's kitten must have drowned with her."

The three young people gasped when they heard that. Mandie knew then why the man was so unhappy. Evidently he had lost a child who had drowned somehow.

"Well, are we going inside now?" Jonathan asked.

Mandie took a deep breath and said, "Come on. Let's go." She headed for the doorway. Jonathan followed and Celia tagged behind.

Pushing open the door, Mandie stepped inside the dirty cabin. The man's furious expression when he saw her stopped her in her tracks.

"Get off my boat!" he yelled at the three. "I told you before. This is my home! Begone!" He stood up to confront them. At that moment Snowball jumped down from his grasp and went straight to Mandie. The man watched.

"This is my kitten," Mandie said as she stooped and picked up Snowball.

The man's expression softened. "He is so much like my baby's kitten."

"I'm terribly sorry your baby drowned," Mandie said. The man looked at her in surprise. "How did you know . . ." He paused.

"We heard you tell Snowball," Mandie replied as she cuddled the kitten. "How did it happen, sir?"

The man frowned and looked as though he would attack them all. "That is not your business!" he snapped. Advancing toward them from across the room, he shook his fist and waved his hands. "Get off my ship and don't come back. And do not allow your cat to come in here again. Do you understand?"

"But, mister, I just wanted to talk to you for a minute," Mandie insisted as she bravely stood her ground. "The short dark man who visits you—did you know the police arrested him and then he must have escaped because we saw him here earlier today."

The big man was plainly shocked. Then he spoke vehemently, "No, that cannot be. In jail? No, no!"

"The newspaper," Mandie said, turning to her friends. "Do y'all have it?"

Jonathan shook his head. "We must have laid it down somewhere."

"I'm pretty sure we left it on the park bench when we cracked the nuts," Celia spoke up.

"Oh, well," Mandie said, turning back to the man. "His picture was on the front page of the newspaper today."

The man frowned again thoughtfully. Then he suddenly shouted at Mandie, "You lie! He cannot be in jail! Get off my boat! Begone!" He advanced toward them again.

Frightened, Mandie and her friends rushed to the rope ladder. The man followed them all the way, waving his hands in the air. He stood there watching as they reached the pier and ran toward the street. Then as Mandie looked back, she saw him go back to his cabin.

Mandie and her friends finally paused in front of a shop to get their breath as they glanced around.

"Mandie, I don't think we ought to go on that man's boat anymore," Celia said as she straightened her long skirts.

"We'll just find a policeman and tell him everything," Mandie said. She looked up and down the street. "Come on. There must be one somewhere."

They walked faster as Mandie determinedly searched for a policeman. People strolled everywhere, and several carriages passed them, but no law officer could be seen.

"Let's go through the tunnel. Remember there were two policemen in there when we were in that room," Mandie said to her friends as she picked up Snowball and turned down the alleyway toward the entrance to the tunnel. She rushed ahead.

"No stopping at that room again!" Jonathan called to her as he and Celia followed.

Mandie ignored his remark as she entered the tunnel.

Not a soul was in sight, and as she came to the doorway of the room leading into the smaller room full of boxes, she paused. No one had bothered anything. She wanted to just run inside, glance around, and come back out into the tunnel.

But she continued down the passageway. As she left the tunnel, she glanced back to be sure her friends were following. She wasn't watching where she was going and ran smack into someone. Snowball protested at the end of his leash.

"Oh, I'm sorry," Mandie began as she looked up. One of the two policemen they had seen earlier stood before her. He smiled at her. "We were just looking for—" She stopped short, then went racing across the wide avenue.

Walking up the other side of the street was her old Cherokee friend, Uncle Ned. He had arrived at last.

"Uncle Ned! Uncle Ned!" she called to him.

He stopped and turned to look back. With a big smile on his face he waited for her to get to his side of the avenue. Celia and Jonathan had also seen him and were hurrying to catch up.

"Uncle Ned, I'm so glad to see you!" she cried as she ran up to the tall Indian and grasped his hand. "We've got all kinds of mysteries that we need you to help us solve."

"Papoose always in mystery," Uncle Ned said, smiling down at her as he squeezed her small hand. "What is mystery this time?"

They were near the park where they had cracked the nuts. Mandie saw that the bench was still empty and she pointed to it. "Let's go sit over there where we can talk a minute."

Jonathan and Celia finally reached them and exchanged greetings with Uncle Ned. Then they all walked back across the street to sit on the park bench.

"You see, it's like this," Mandie began as she started a jumbled account of what had been happening.

Celia spied the newspaper on the ground near the bench and picked it up and gave it to Mandie.

"Uncle Ned, see this man's picture? We've been seeing him all over town," Mandie said, holding the newspaper out to Uncle Ned. "We saw him in the hotel with the painting and all those other places I told you about; and according to this paper, they arrested him, but we saw him after that down at the old boat."

"Take breath, Papoose. I listen slow," the old Indian told her as he patted her hand. "We find what's wrong. We go see." He stood up.

Mandie rose and looked up into his wrinkled face. "When did you get here, Uncle Ned? Where is your baggage?" She carried the newspaper with her this time.

"Bag already at hotel, room next to Jonathan. Just now," Uncle Ned replied. "Horse in stable."

"Horse? You brought your horse?" Jonathan asked excitedly.

"Yes, pay money to ride horse from Germany," Uncle Ned explained.

"Oh, you rented the horse," Celia spoke up.

"Well, I didn't think you rode a horse from the United States," Mandie said with a giggle. "But you've had a horse everywhere you go."

"Give back horse and ride ship home with Papoose," Uncle Ned said, smiling at her. "Keep Papoose out of trouble."

The three young people laughed.

"That's impossible, Uncle Ned, to keep Mandie out of trouble, you know that," Jonathan said, with his mischievous grin.

Mandie looked at the boy and said, "You do pretty well yourself getting into trouble, like falling in the water at the pier." She grinned.

"Oh, Mandie, stop bringing that up or I'll begin reminding you of all your escapades," Jonathan warned.

"Go," Uncle Ned told them.

"We'll go by the tunnel room first since that's on the way, and then we'll take you to the old boat," Mandie explained as she walked along beside him. Her friends loved Uncle Ned, too, and they stayed close by on the other side of him.

"Where grandmother of Papoose?" Uncle Ned asked as they crossed the street.

Mandie held the newspaper in one hand and Snowball in the other and explained, "She and Senator Morton have been gone to a reception all day and won't be back until later this afternoon." She looked up at the old Indian and added, "So we've been free all day."

Uncle Ned looked down at her as they walked along. "Papoose must learn to be trustworthy. Grandmother of Papoose trust Papoose."

"But, Uncle Ned, we haven't done anything really bad," Mandie replied with a smile. Then she frowned as she remembered the argument with her grandmother and she added, "I've been guilty of other things, though, and I need to talk to you as soon as we get a chance."

Uncle Ned looked at her thoughtfully. "Yes, Papoose must tell what bothers her."

When they arrived at the room in the tunnel and showed the boxes to Uncle Ned he told them, "Boxes belong to somebody. Papoose must not bother other people's belongings. Must pay for smashed boxes." He looked at her with a frown.

"But, Uncle Ned, like I told you, these boxes must

belong to some smuggler, or thief, or something. Who else would pack up rocks in boxes?" Mandie asked as she walked about the room with her two friends.

"That business of police, not Papoose," Uncle Ned reminded her. "This foreign land. We Americans. We not mess with police business."

Mandie shrugged. "Come on. We'll go on to the old boat."

The young people were surprised to see how agile Uncle Ned was as he quickly climbed the rope ladders and stepped onto the deck of the boat. Mandie knew he was awfully old and that he could do practically anything, but she had never seen him so active before. And he had carried his bow and arrows in the sling across the shoulder of his deerskin jacket as he boarded the vessel.

"Sh-h-h!" Mandie cautioned them as they crept behind the trash pile and Uncle Ned joined them. She held Snowball tightly in her arms.

Uncle Ned glanced around the boat from their hiding place. Mandie started to whisper to him, but at that moment a loud sob from inside the cabin filled the air. Alex was crying his heart out again. The young people listened and watched Uncle Ned to see what his reaction was. A worried expression covered his face.

"There's a window," Mandie whispered to her Cherokee friend. She pointed, handed Snowball and the newspaper to Celia, and began moving in a crouched position toward the cabin. Uncle Ned looked puzzled and then he followed her.

At the window Mandie could see Alex lying on the bunk bed. She looked back and motioned for Celia to let Snowball come to her. The kitten raced toward his mistress and then changed his mind and slipped through the cracked door. Mandie and Uncle Ned watched through the window as Snowball didn't even hesitate this time but jumped upon the bed and stuck his face next to Alex's and began loudly meowing. Alex tried to push him away, but he clung to the mattress with his claws.

Alex sat up and picked up Snowball. "You insist on bothering me. If you didn't look so much like my baby's kitten, I'd throw you overboard. That I would." Alex stroked Snowball's fur as the kitten climbed up to hang on his shoulder.

"The Lord has forsaken me," Alex moaned. "I am so guilty! I killed my family!" He broke into uncontrollable sobs as he sat there. Snowball squirmed until he released him, and the kitten jumped down and ran back outside to his mistress.

"Killed his family?" Mandie almost screamed when she heard that. She looked up at Uncle Ned. "He must be a murderer!"

Uncle Ned didn't answer but kept watching the man. Jonathan and Celia had crept up behind them and now Celia reached for Mandie's hand.

"Let's go, Mandie," Celia whispered. "He is dangerous. He might kill us." Mandie felt her trembling by her side. She looked back and saw that Jonathan had taken Celia's other hand and was trying to comfort her.

Suddenly the man bellowed, "Oh, God, I am so guilty! Please let me just leave this world! I have nothing to live for!" He shook with sobs.

Mandie tightened her grasp on Uncle Ned's hand and looked at him. He was still intently watching the man inside.

She made a quick decision and whispered to Uncle Ned as she stood up, "I am going inside to talk to him."

Before Uncle Ned could stop her, Mandie had entered the cabin and stood before the man, who didn't see her at first. She walked closer. He finally looked up but his eyes stared blankly at her, and he continued to sit on the side of the bunk bed. He didn't rush angrily at her as he had been doing, but acted as though he didn't know she was there.

"Mister Alex," Mandie began as she crept close enough to grasp one of his big hairy hands. "God has not forsaken you. If you believe in Him, He will always be with you—"

Finally Alex realized she was speaking. "God? What do you know about God? He let me have a terrible accident and kill my family. He doesn't love me anymore."

Mandie still held on to his hand and knelt in front of him to get his full attention. "If you had an accident, then it was an accident. You didn't deliberately kill your family like you've been screaming about."

"I did! I did! I let the boat get out of control in that hair-raising storm and I couldn't save them. Oh, my pretty baby, she disappeared. My wife was found too late," he moaned.

"Well, if it was a storm that caused you to have an accident, then you didn't cause the storm. God created it," Mandie tried to explain as she watched his face.

"You're all wrong!" Alex said, suddenly standing up and waving his hands. "Get off my boat! I told you before! Begone!"

Mandie jumped up and backed off toward the door. She wasn't afraid, because she knew Uncle Ned was watching. Snowball had been let loose in the excitement and now he came to his mistress. He hissed and sputtered at the man and raised the hair on his back. Mandie reached down and picked him up.

"Oh, Snowball, behave," she told the kitten. "Mister Alex, please listen to me." She moved around the room instead of leaving. She caught sight of what looked like the packages the other man had been bringing to the boat. They were lined up on a shelf nearby, still wrapped. She managed to grasp one and quickly pulled the paper off. It was a loaf of bread and cheese.

"If you are hungry take the food. I will not eat it. I don't want to live," Alex told her as he watched. "But get off my boat. Now! Begone!"

Mandie quickly replaced the half package on the shelf. "That other man, the one who visits you, has been bringing you food and you're not eating it. You'll starve to death."

"Then that would be a good riddance to the world," Alex told her as he took a handkerchief from his pocket and wiped his eyes.

To Mandie's amazement Uncle Ned had suddenly appeared in the doorway. She watched as he stepped inside. Alex gazed at the old Indian in shock for a moment and then yelled, "Even the Indians bother me. Get off my boat!" He walked toward Uncle Ned and stood facing him. "Begone!"

"Yes, we be gone," Uncle Ned said, reaching for Mandie's hand. "We be gone."

Mandie let Uncle Ned lead her out of the cabin and to the rope ladder as her friends went ahead. When they all arrived at the street at the end of the pier they stopped to talk.

Mandie told them about the bread and cheese, which they hadn't been able to see from the window. "I'm puzzled now about Alex and the other man," she said as they sat on a low wall nearby.

Uncle Ned said, "Man grieving himself to death. Sad, but dangerous. Papoose must not bother man."

"But, Uncle Ned, someone needs to talk to him and

make him understand that he didn't kill his family. It was the storm," Mandie insisted.

"Papoose say other man come to boat, talk to big man," Uncle Ned said. "He come enough times big man will listen to him."

"I have been thinking that man is a thief and that man's picture is in the newspaper," Mandie mused. "It doesn't all make sense. Unless Alex is really a thief, too."

"But that other man has been bringing Alex food," Jonathan said.

"Maybe Alex is just putting on, with the crying and all, trying to make people feel sorry for him and to cover up his meanness," Celia suggested.

"No, that couldn't be, because he cries when there's no one there to hear," Mandie told her.

"Grief real," Uncle Ned said firmly. "Man grieving."

"Well, what can we do, Uncle Ned?" Mandie asked.

Uncle Ned frowned and said, "We think something. Now we go to hotel." He stood up. Mandie rose and grasped his hand.

"Please wait a minute, Uncle Ned," she said. Turning to her friends, she said, "Do y'all mind if I stay here a few minutes more and talk to Uncle Ned about something else that's bothering me? We'll only be a few minutes."

"Sure, Mandie, we'll go on back," Jonathan agreed. "I'll walk Snowball back for you." He took the end of the kitten's leash.

"If your grandmother has returned, we'll tell her where you are," Celia said as she and Jonathan went off up the street, with Snowball trying to run ahead. "I have the newspaper." She held it up.

Mandie and Uncle Ned sat back down. She didn't know exactly how to begin. Uncle Ned silently waited.

"Uncle Ned, I've been bad, terribly bad with my grandmother, and I don't know how to fix things," Mandie began, with a quiver in her voice.

"Bad?" the old Indian questioned as she paused.

"You see, my grandmother and I had an awful argument and she's still mad at me," Mandie continued. "Neither one of us mentions the argument but there is a . . . a . . . strain, I guess you'd call it, between us since then."

"Tell about argument, Papoose," Uncle Ned said, watching her closely.

Mandie related what had occurred between her grandmother and her because she had touched the muslin in the museum. She placed the blame on herself. She realized now that she shouldn't say mean things back when someone said something to her that she didn't like. She should have just ignored it.

"I really love my grandmother, Uncle Ned, regardless of what happened years ago," Mandie said, tears filling her blue eyes. "And I'm afraid I've caused her not to love me anymore."

Uncle Ned put an arm around Mandie's thin shoulders. "Papoose did wrong. Papoose must tell grandmother sorry. Must ask forgiveness."

"I'll try, Uncle Ned, but when I went to her room and intended apologizing, I just couldn't make myself say a word about it," Mandie said.

"Grandmother also wrong. Need tell Papoose she sorry," Uncle Ned said.

Mandie looked at him in surprise. "Why was my grandmother wrong?"

"Grandmother should not say bad things about Jim Shaw that upset Papoose," the old Indian tried to explain. "Grandmother must forgive, too, because she was one who caused problem at start by separating mother of Papoose and Jim Shaw. Must all forgive each other. And

Papoose must ask Big God forgive her."

Mandie leaned close to the old Indian as his arm tightened about her shoulders; and as he raised his face toward the sky, she knew he was waiting for her to follow suit.

Looking at the white clouds sailing high in the blue sky, Mandie saw God in her mind, sitting at His window and looking down on the world. She could feel His love as a tremor ran through her. "Dear God, please forgive me for hurting my grandmother. I'm sorry." Tears blurred her vision and she added, "Thank you, dear God, thank you."

"Thank you, Big God," Uncle Ned repeated after her.

Mandie turned to put her arms around the old Indian in a quick hug, and said, "And, thank you, Uncle Ned. I love you. Please don't ever get old and die and leave me."

Uncle Ned smiled as they stood up. "We must all go see Big God one day," he said. "Jim Shaw up there in happy hunting ground waiting for us."

"I know," Mandie said softly as she looked back up at the sky.

As they walked toward the hotel, Mandie felt as though a burden had been lifted off her small shoulders. She wanted to get back and talk to her grandmother.

And she also wanted to talk with her friends about what they would do next concerning Alex, the room full of boxes, and the other man. But at least now she had Uncle Ned to help her solve this mystery.

Chapter 12 / Unexpected Happenings

When Mandie and Uncle Ned arrived back at the hotel, Celia and Jonathan were waiting for them in the reception room. Snowball's leash was tied to a chair leg and he was curled up asleep on the rug. Celia still had the newspaper.

"Is my grandmother back?" Mandie asked as she and Uncle Ned approached her friends.

"No, not yet," Jonathan said as he turned around to look at the front door. "But here she comes now with Senator Morton." He motioned toward the door.

Mrs. Taft and Senator Morton hurried inside, then stopped abruptly when they saw everyone waiting for them.

"Well, well, quite a reception committee," Senator Morton said, laughing. He reached to shake hands with Uncle Ned. "Good to see you again, sir."

"And you," Uncle Ned replied as Mrs. Taft also greeted him.

"I'm so glad you finally caught up with us. I feel the young people are so much safer with you around, Uncle Ned."

The old Indian smiled and dropped his gaze. He never knew how to react to a compliment.

"What are you planning now, Grandmother?" Mandie eagerly asked as they all stood there.

Before she could answer, Jonathan spoke up. "Senator Morton, there's a message to you from my aunt and uncle at the desk. It came this morning."

"I'll get it," the senator said, going over to the desk clerk.

"Amanda, before we discuss any plans, let's all get cleaned up and take a little walk before supper," Mrs. Taft told her. "We've been cooped up all day without any exercise and all that food—I just couldn't resist it."

Senator Morton rejoined them with two pieces of paper in his hand. "I also received a wire from your father, Jonathan," the senator said, extending a piece of paper to the boy. "Read it if you'd like." Turning to Mrs. Taft he said, "His father would like him to travel on with us. He's unable to catch up with us right now. And his aunt and uncle are going back out of town again."

Jonathan read the message and handed it back to the senator. He tried not to look disappointed as he said, "He must have known we haven't solved the mystery here yet and that Mandie would need my help."

Mrs. Taft quickly looked at her granddaughter. "Amanda," she said as she sank into a nearby chair, "what have y'all been up to while we were gone?"

Jonathan grimaced as he realized he had given away their secret. Mandie gave him an exasperated look.

"This man on the old boat down at the far end of the pier is in bad shape, Grandmother. He needs our help,"

Mandie said as she leaned toward her grandmother. "The police caught the man who stole the paintings, but he escaped and has been going down to see the man on the boat—"

"Amanda! What on earth are you talking about?" Mrs. Taft interrupted impatiently. She looked at Uncle Ned and asked, "What have they been into now?"

The old Indian shook his head and looked at Mandie. "Papoose must tell you," he said.

"All right, Amanda, let's go on up to my room," Mrs. Taft said, rising from the chair. She told the others, "We'll meet here again in about thirty minutes, if that's all right with y'all."

The others agreed as they all went toward the elevator. Mandie carried her kitten.

Celia looked at Mandie and said, "I'll take Snowball on up to our rooms for you. And I still have the newspaper." She waved it at Mandie.

"Thanks, Celia," Mandie said, handing Snowball to her.

As Mrs. Taft opened the door to her suite and Mandie followed her inside, Mandie was suddenly overcome with emotion. Mrs. Taft sat down nearby as she removed her hat. Mandie ran to kneel before her and hold her hands.

"Grandmother, I'm sorry for the way I've acted with you, the argument about my father. Please forgive me. I do really and truly love you," Mandie said, tears flooding her blue eyes.

To her surprise Mrs. Taft pulled her up onto her lap and hugged her tight. As the lady spoke, Mandie noticed that her voice quivered. "Amanda, I was wrong, too. Please forgive me. I am awfully headstrong sometimes. That's probably where you get your unpredictable impulses. I love you, too, dear, with all my heart."

Mandie leaned back to smile at her grandmother and saw tears streaming down her cheeks. Reaching in her pocket Mandie pulled out her handkerchief and said, "Here, Grandmother, you first and then me." Her voice shook. She reached up and dried her grandmother's face and then wiped her own eyes.

Mrs. Taft gave her a little push off her lap. "I'm afraid you've got too big to hold like that," she said with a little laugh.

"I know I have. I was about to fall off," Mandie said with a grin. She sat on the carpet in front of her grandmother's chair.

"Now that we've both forgiven each other, what was this about that man on the boat?" Mrs. Taft asked.

"His name is Alex. He needs our help, Grandmother," Mandie said, and then she suddenly had a bright idea. "Grandmother, I know how you've helped a lot of people, like Violet and Lily on the ship, and Hilda back home, and all the others. Alex is all alone and has no one to help him, or love him. He lost his wife and his little girl in an accident on his boat during a bad storm, and he blames himself for it. And the man who's been visiting him and taking him food was arrested by the police for stealing the paintings and—"

"Amanda, dear, please start at the beginning. You are not making any sense at all," Mrs. Taft told her with a slight smile.

"Sorry, Grandmother," Mandie said, and she related their entire adventures. She wanted to wipe the slate clean between them, and she didn't want to hold anything back.

Mrs. Taft listened with a frown and a gasp now and then. When Mandie finished she said, "Amanda, Uncle Ned is right. The stolen paintings are the police's business. And if this man Alex is connected with that, then we need to ask the police to look into—"

"Excuse me, Grandmother, but—" Mandie interrupted.

Mrs. Taft interrupted her. "However, if the man is innocent of any wrongdoing, I'll be glad to do whatever I can for him. But we must be sure he is not connected with the theft."

Mandie sighed. "All right, Grandmother. But how are we going to do that?"

Mrs. Taft stood up, smiled, and said, "As you're always saying, we'll find a way. Now go get cleaned up so we won't keep the others waiting."

Mandie jumped to her feet, quickly planted a kiss on her grandmother's cheek, and ran for the door. "I'll be ready in five minutes. I love you." She was out the door and gone before Mrs. Taft could reply.

Mandie felt lighthearted. She ran into the rooms she shared with Celia and found her friend already putting on clean clothes. Snowball was asleep on the bed.

"Grandmother is going to help us solve our mystery," Mandie said in a singsong as she ran for the wardrobe to get a clean dress.

Celia whirled around and looked at her friend in surprise.

"Your grandmother? You told her everything?" Celia asked in disbelief.

Mandie smiled and said, "Yes, everything. And she's going to help us find out whether Alex is a crook or not; and if he isn't, then she's going to help him."

"Help him?" Celia asked.

"With all her money she could help lots and lots of people," Mandie replied as she pulled off her dress.

"But, Mandie, it isn't just money Alex needs," Celia reminded her.

"I know, but Grandmother always thinks in terms of money. So we can let her supply the money and we'll do the rest, like trying to help him overcome his guilt problem," Mandie said, rushing into the bathroom to wash up.

When the girls were ready to leave the rooms, Mandie looked at Snowball fast asleep in the middle of her bed. He was probably worn out by all the activity that day.

"Are you taking Snowball?" Celia asked.

"I think I'll take a chance and let him sleep, but I'll move him into the bathroom and shut the door," Mandie said, rushing to put a pillow on the bathroom floor and then returning to take him in there and place him on the pillow. Snowball didn't even wake up all the way as she picked him up. He opened one blue eye, looked up at his mistress, and slept right on.

"He is tired. He didn't even protest," Mandie said as she closed the door.

The girls rushed downstairs to join the others and found they were the first ones there. They sat on a nearby settee, and Mandie glanced at the newspaper she had brought with her.

"This must be an awfully smart man to escape jail so soon after they arrested him," Mandie remarked, looking at the photo on the front page. "But then I suppose thieves have to be smart like that."

Jonathan came into the room. "We young ones sure do get around fast, don't we?" He looked around at other guests of the hotel in the reception room.

"Not really fast. Here come Grandmother and Senator Morton and Uncle Ned now," Mandie said with a grin.

Mrs. Taft spoke to Mandie. "Uncle Ned and Senator Morton and I have discussed things and have decided you young people should show the senator and me this room with the boxes and the old boat." She smiled. "Now let's go."

Mandie was surprised, but she smiled at her grandmother as she and her friends led the way. She held on to the newspaper.

When they reached the entrance to the tunnel, the young people paused for the older ones to catch up with them.

"The room with the boxes is in here," Mandie explained as she opened the door and went inside.

They soon came to the room that opened into the one with the boxes. Mandie opened the first door and found the door to the inner room standing open. As she hurried to inspect the boxes, she could see that nothing had been disturbed. The small painting was still lying where the man had left it when they saw him in the room.

"You see all these rocks? They were packed in straw in the wooden boxes that we broke open there," Mandie explained to her grandmother. "And this little painting was inside another box we opened."

Mrs. Taft quickly looked at the painting. "This looks like an original, but I don't see a signature on it anywhere." She examined it closely.

"We couldn't find one either," Jonathan spoke up.

Mrs. Taft looked at the senator and asked, "Do you have a knife? I believe this frame has been put over the signature."

Senator Morton didn't have a knife but Uncle Ned did, and he carefully pried the corner of the frame loose. Mrs. Taft was right. There was a name on the corner of the painting.

"Moire? Hmmm, I don't recognize that name as belonging to any artist I've ever heard of, but then I haven't heard of all the artists whose works are worth money,"

Mrs. Taft said as she touched the signature with her finger.

"Neither have I," Senator Morton agreed as he took the painting and inspected it. Then he pushed the frame back together and laid the painting down where they had found it.

"All right now, let's go on," Mrs. Taft told the young people.

Mandie led the way to the old boat. She was secretly wondering how her grandmother could ever get up the rope ladders and onto the boat. But as the pier came in sight, she knew that problem was solved. Alex was walking down the pier toward the street.

"There's Alex!" she said excitedly, pointing to the man in the distance.

"I wonder what made him leave his boat," Jonathan remarked as they walked on.

Mandie watched as they came closer. She saw Alex come to the end of the pier and then walk to his left. She knew there was a small park in that direction and she figured that was where he was headed. And she was right. He stepped off the street into the grassy section and sat down on a nearby bench.

Mandie dropped back to speak to her grandmother. "Look, that man on the bench over there. That's Alex. Something has caused him to leave the boat," she said excitedly.

"Then we'll go talk to him in the park," Mrs. Taft said, heading in that direction.

When they approached the man, the adults stayed back until the young people had made him aware of their presence.

"Mister Alex, I'm so glad you came out for a walk," Mandie said as she advanced toward him. Jonathan and Celia stayed right behind her.

Alex looked surprised and at a loss for words for a moment. Then he asked, "Where is that white kitten?"

"Oh, Snowball was so tired and sleepy, we left him back at the hotel," Mandie explained as she and her friends came closer.

"And what be you wanting this time?" Alex asked as he glanced back and saw the adults coming in his direction.

Mandie held out the newspaper and said, "I wanted you to see this newspaper, for one thing. That's your friend's picture on the front page and—"

Alex took the paper, looked at it, and immediately said in a loud voice, "That is not my friend! Once and for all, that is not my friend!" He threw the paper at Mandie.

"That's the same man who comes to see you on the boat," Mandie insisted as she picked up the newspaper.

The adults had stopped to listen. And suddenly Mandie was aware of a policeman standing nearby. She had not seen him come up.

"Is something wrong?" the policeman asked Mandie.

Mandie held the newspaper out to him. "This man on the front page comes to visit this man called Alex here on his boat down there. We've seen him several times."

"We have arrested that man for stealing paintings," the policeman told her. He looked at Alex. "I do not know anything about this man on the bench."

"They are friends. When this man you arrested escaped, he came to Alex's boat. We saw him," Mandie insisted.

The policeman looked at her in surprise. "The man in the paper there whom we arrested is still in jail. I just left him after an hour of interrogation. He will not tell us what he has done with the paintings, but he is still in jail."

Mandie and her friends looked at one another, puzzled.

"Well?" she said.

Suddenly Alex stood up. They turned to look at him. The short dark man who had visited him was approaching from the street.

Mandie thought, *Uh-huh, we'll prove to the policeman that the dark man coming here is the same one.* The officer was also watching the man as he drew nearer.

The short dark man ignored them and went straight to Alex and put an arm around his shoulders. "Oh, Alex, this is in answer to my prayers, to see you out like this." He sat down as Alex did.

Mandie shook the newspaper at the policeman and said, "You see that man there? He's the same one whose picture is in the newspaper. Look!"

The policeman glanced at the paper and then at the dark man.

"Miss, you would never make a policeman. Don't you see the different hairline on this man and the one in the paper? His ears stick out," he explained to the young people.

The three moved nearer to examine their suspect on the bench. He smiled up at them.

"I am glad to see you again," the man said. "And isn't it wonderful that the Lord has spoken to Alex and caused him to come off that wrecked boat?"

"What an incorrect statement, my friend," Alex said. "It was the beautiful young lady there with the blond hair and blue, blue eyes who persuaded me to reassess my guilt." He smiled at Mandie.

Mandie gasped. "You mean what I said helped you? Oh, it's almost too good to believe!" She smiled at him as tears of joy filled her eyes.

The adults had stood back, listening and watching. Now Mrs. Taft walked forward.

"This is my granddaughter," she said to Alex. "She told me you might need a little help, perhaps to get your boat repaired so you can work again. You are a fisherman, aren't you?"

Alex and his friend had stood up. "I was a fisherman, madam. However, my minister friend runs an orphanage, and he has been after me for a long time to come and work with him, and that's what I've decided to do," Alex explained with a big smile. "I thank you for your concern."

Mandie watched to see what her grandmother would do. The policeman was still standing there, too. She went to whisper to Uncle Ned, "I hope she gives the orphanage some money."

Uncle Ned smiled and squeezed her hand.

Mandie was right. Her grandmother was saying, "Oh, but an orphanage can always use some extra money." She turned to the minister. "Would you care to come to the hotel where we are staying and let's discuss this matter?"

"Of course, madam," the minister said, smiling broadly.

The policeman approached Mandie and said, "That settles your question, doesn't it now? There are two different men who look a great deal alike."

"Yes, sir, but we know something else you might like to hear about," Mandie said as she looked at Jonathan and Celia, who crowded close.

"And what is that, may I ask?" the policeman said.

"You told us the man you arrested wouldn't tell you where he hid the paintings. We think we know, don't we?" She turned to her two friends and they both nodded.

"And where is that? And how do you know about this?" the policeman asked. He was looking over the three young people and added, "Americans, are you?"

"Yes, sir," all three answered.

"We found a room full of boxes," Mandie began. "We broke open three of the boxes. Two of them had nothing but rocks and straw inside. The third box had a small painting inside it."

The policeman got excited immediately. "Where? Where is this place you are talking about?"

"In the tunnel that comes out down this way," Mandie pointed.

"Show me," the policeman demanded.

Mrs. Taft and the other adults had been talking and now they stopped to listen.

"Grandmother, this policeman wants to see the room in the tunnel," Mandie told her.

"Very well. We'll walk back that way," Mrs. Taft agreed. She turned to Alex and the minister. "Are you coming along?"

"Yes, madam," they both said as they followed Mrs. Taft, Senator Morton, and Uncle Ned.

The young people went ahead with the policeman.

As they all stood around the room in the tunnel watching the policeman examine things, everyone was excited about the way it had all turned out.

"Yes, miss, I'd say some smuggling has been going on here," the policeman said to Mandie. "We'll let you know as soon as we have opened the other boxes."

"I certainly would like to know that the thief has been caught and you were able to recover the stolen paintings," Mandie told him.

"We will walk back to the hotel now. The policeman can find us there if he needs to," Mrs. Taft said.

"Yes, madam," the policeman agreed as he continued moving boxes around.

Then Mandie remembered something and she told

the officer, "There were two policemen here once before. They found the door open and mentioned some man's name, but we couldn't understand what it was."

"Thank you. I will find out," the man said.

As the young people walked along behind the adults, Mandie remarked, "What about that? The man was a minister all the time and I thought he was a thief."

"You can't judge too much from appearances sometimes. He doesn't look as if he has much money," Jonathan said in a low voice.

"I know," Mandie whispered. "And I hope Grandmother gives him a big chunk of hers for the orphanage."

The young people waited with Uncle Ned in the reception room while Mrs. Taft, Senator Morton, and the two men discussed business in the tea parlor.

"Oh, this has all turned out so wonderful this time," Mandie remarked to her friends.

Jonathan and Celia smiled.

"There is more to come," Uncle Ned told them.

The three were instantly curious.

"What?" they all asked.

"Big reward for finding paintings," Uncle Ned told them.

The three looked at one another with big eyes; then as though reading one another's thoughts, they simultaneously shook their heads.

"We don't want the money," Mandie said, and her friends nodded in agreement.

"Orphanage can use lots of money," the old Indian reminded them.

"Of course. That's what we'll do with it if they give us a reward, won't we?" she asked her friends.

"Right," Jonathan agreed.

"Yes," Celia said. "Those poor children always need money."

Mandie looked back at Uncle Ned. "Are you going to Holland with us?"

Uncle Ned nodded. "Yes, must watch over Papoose and her mysteries. Big mystery in Holland."

"There is? How do you know?" Mandie asked quickly.

"What is it?" Jonathan wanted to know.

"Here we go again," said Celia.

Uncle Ned continued to smile and said, "Would not be mystery if I tell you what it is. Must be patient. Wait and see."

"Now you have us so curious, we'll be counting the minutes until we get to Holland," Mandie said with a big smile.

"Count minutes to tomorrow. Leave then for Holland," Uncle Ned replied.

"Tomorrow! Oh, that's great!" Mandie exclaimed.

That night she and Celia lay awake discussing their adventures in Antwerp. And they played a guessing game as to what the mystery in Holland would be, and whether that strange woman from the ship would also turn up in that country.